The Adventures of Rob

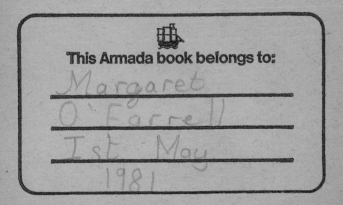

This Armada book belongs to:

Margaret
O'Farrell
Ist May
1981

Author's note:

Since I was about four years old I've been fascinated by the legend of Robin Hood. Writing a book on Robin Hood led me back to the original ballads about him that for many years were passed on by word of mouth before they were written down. I've based my book on these ballads with echoes from the days when the trees in my school playground were Sherwood Forest and playtime was filled with the imaginary adventures of the outlaws.

The Adventures of Robin Hood

Patricia Leitch

Illustrated by Peter Archer

An Armada Original

The Adventures of Robin Hood was first published in the U.K.
in 1979 in Armada by Fontana Paperbacks,
14 St. James's Place, London SW1A 1PS

© Patricia Leitch 1979

Printed in Great Britain by
Love and Malcomson Ltd., Brighton Road,
Redhill, Surrey.

CHAPTER ONE

Green and grey were the colours of Sherwood in the May dawn. Greens of new leaves and grasses, green light filtering through the branches of the high forest trees, and grey dawn-mists breathing out of the dense undergrowth to spiral and wisp into the sky. All promising warmth and growth.

Through the mists came three deer – a fallow buck followed by two does. They came to the edge of a clearing in the trees, stepping delicately, glistening eyes wide and fan ears tense for the least sound.

A boy stood at the roots of a great oak tree, watching them. He was twelve years of age, lean and lithe. His thick hair was brown and wavy, his eyes bright with hazel lights, and the line of his lips was strong and firm. His skin was tanned dark as leather, yet his clothes showed that he was no peasant but the son of a rich man. The boy's name was Robert Fitzooth, known to his family and friends as Robin. His father was the Earl of Huntingdon, whose estates lay close to Bryunsdale, a part of the great forest of Sherwood in Nottinghamshire.

Even when Robin was standing still you could sense the energy in him. As he stood, hardly breathing, his eyes fixed on the deer, you knew how he could run and leap and climb; sit close on a galloping horse; dance nimbly about his opponent when wrestling, and withstand the clash and thrust of another's staff. All these things you knew, as you know, looking at a roosting hawk, how it can soar and plunge.

On Robin's back was slung a longbow, not the full size of a man's bow but longer than the bow carried by many a youth. A full quiver of arrows hung from his shoulder.

The wind blew from the deer towards Robin so that they did not scent him. The buck, his head held high, stepped cautiously into the clearing. He paused, nostrils drinking the wind for any breath of danger. Robin's hand closed on the end of his bow. His other hand itched to fit an arrow into the bowstring and send it straight into the buck's heart. The deer was within easy range and Robin knew that if he shot at it the beast was his, but he clenched his hands tight, nails biting into his palm, to stop himself.

It was the reign of King Henry II. Sherwood was a royal forest; not only the massive woodlands but every field and village within the forest was controlled by the King's Foresters, and anyone found killing the King's deer would be taken to one of the King's special courts and brutally sentenced. Robin released his hold on his bow. From the servants in his father's Hall he had heard too many terrifying tales of the kind of justice that was dealt out to anyone found shooting the King's game to want to test the truth for himself.

Suddenly Robin's quick eye saw a movement on the other side of the clearing. Two peasants, a man, and a boy, about the same age as Robin, were standing more than half hidden in the dense undergrowth. The man had a scarlet handkerchief knotted round his arm and as he strung an arrow to his bow the flash of scarlet had caught Robin's eye. Almost before Robin realised what was happening the man's arrow was buried deep in the heart of the buck. The beast crumpled to its knees, its head tipped forward, antlers ploughing the turf, and it fell, a dead bulk, in the clearing. The does had long since vanished.

Grasping a knife in his hand, the man, closely followed by the boy, dashed forward to his quarry. Now that Robin could see them clearly it was obvious why they had dared to break the King's laws. On their faces were clear marks of a winter's starvation. Their eyes were set in gaunt

6

sockets, their cheeks clamped flat and hollow, and from their ragged sleeves their wrists and hands hung down like skeletons' jangling bones.

"Now mother will get better," cried the boy. "Now we will have soup and meat and she will get well again." His white face gazed anxiously at his father.

But the man was too concerned with the dead deer to reassure his son. He knelt over the beast, slitting its belly with a sure stroke of his knife, and all the time, as he worked, he looked about him with quick, nervous glances. He knew only too well that the deer were guarded by the King's Foresters. Few of the Foresters dared to go into the deep heart of Sherwood, fearing the outlaws who made their homes there, but here, only a few miles from one of the roads that crossed through Sherwood, the Foresters were everywhere. If they found him, his death or mutilation was certain. His own cousin, who had only been suspected of shooting a deer, had had his right hand cut off at the wrist.

The thought made the man shudder violently but he remembered his wife, lying at home with a wasting fever. He gritted his teeth and got on with the work of disembowelling the buck. His wife had known where he was going and had tied her red handkerchief round his arm to bring him luck. He glanced at it now and took fresh courage from it, but his heart was bitter. He hated the King and all his barons and the corrupt bishops and priests who demanded taxes and tithes from all the peasants. The taxes were so high that when they were paid there was not enough money left to buy food to keep a man's family alive through the winter. Every year, men, women and children died of starvation, while all about them the forests were filled with deer and boar – nature's gift of food to every man; not just to the King alone, or to his barons, but the birthright of every Englishman.

There was a sound close to the edge of the clearing. The

7

man froze, his head turned towards the danger. Hidden by the trunk of the oak, Robin heard it too. Someone was pushing their way through the undergrowth. From the opposite side of the clearing came similar sounds. The man grabbed his son by the arm and, abandoning their kill, they ran across the short grass into the shelter of the trees.

A man in the livery of the King's Foresters burst into the clearing. He was swarthy and thick-set. His glance took in the newly-killed deer and he looked sharply round the trees and undergrowth. Another man dressed in the same livery came running to join him.

"Too late. They have gone," swore the first, and he kicked at the carcass lying at his feet. Then a glimpse of scarlet caught his eye.

"Yet not so," he yelled as he charged into the trees. "We have them."

In seconds the man and the boy were overpowered; the man so weak that he could hardly struggle; the boy too young to do more than shout and kick hopelessly against his captors.

"Kill the King's deer, you vermin," cried the thick-set Forester. "We shall see how you like the taste of this venison. We shall see if you can taste it at all when the Sheriff's men have dealt with you."

"My wife is dying for lack of food. It was for her that I killed the deer."

"He admits it!" cried the second Forester, who had ginger whiskers and a nervous twitch in his right eye. "In front of us, he admits his own guilt."

"Let my son go," pleaded the man. "Do what you like with me but set the boy free. He had no part in this."

In answer, the dark Forester threw the boy to the ground and kept him there with a booted foot on his neck.

"No part in it?" he demanded, his red face pushed close to the man's. "Tell that to the Sheriff."

8

"Send him back to his mother," beseeched the man desperately. "He is but a child."

"Keep your wretched snivelling to yourself," and the Forester hit the man about the head.

Hidden from the men by the undergrowth, Robin had climbed, swiftly and silently, into the branches of the oak tree. From his perch he watched intently. He had cried out in rage when he had seen the Forester hit the peasant but they had not heard him.

The Foresters tied the hands and feet of their prisoners and left them on the ground beside the dead deer.

"Stay here to guard them," ordered the dark Forester. "I shall go to the nearest village, bring back a cart for the deer and we will take them all to Nottingham for the justice they deserve."

"Do not be gone too long," said the foxy Forester who was to be left behind.

"Afraid of a bound man and a boy?" taunted his companion.

"That I am not, but of the outlaws who roam these forests." He stared round apprehensively. "No man walks here alone."

"You have your bow."

"Aye, and what use one bow against a band of reckless cut-throats and thieves? You leave me here like a bait to lure them to me."

"Do you refuse to stay? I think our master, the Sheriff of Nottingham, will be interested to know what a brave man he has to serve him."

"Go if you must. But only a fool waits alone in Sherwood. Waste no more time."

"A fool and a coward!" mocked the Forester as he set off into the trees.

When the sound of his jeering laughter had died away the ginger-whiskered Forester checked on his prisoners' bonds then sat down on the ground to wait.

In the oak, Robin waited as well, and although his hazel eyes twinkled with mischief his mouth was set in a firm line of determination. A little while later, he slipped, as silent as a shadow, down into the lower branches of the oak. He fitted an arrow to his bow and drew back his bowstring to send the arrow buzzing like a wasp straight to its target – a spot on the ground little more than an inch from the Forester's foot.

Almost before the arrow had hit the ground Robin had dropped from the oak to run silently round the clearing and send another arrow singing past the Forester's ear as he struggled to his feet. A third arrow followed, coming from another part of the forest trees. The man and the boy watched from where they lay on the ground, hope lighting their faces for the first time since they had been captured.

Robin's fourth arrow lodged in the point of the Forester's hood. Trembling with fear, the man fell to his knees.

"Varlet," cried Robin, lowering his voice so that the warder would not guess that he was only a boy. "My men surround you. Do as I command or our arrows will find your heart."

"Take pity. Do not shoot! Tell me what you want. I am a poor man. I only work for the Sheriff. A man must find work where he can . . ."

"Untie your prisoners and set them free," commanded Robin's voice.

"I dare not. When Will Broothern comes back and finds them gone . . ."

Another arrow from Robin's bow lodged beside its fellow in the Forester's hood.

"At once," commanded Robin.

With shaking hands the Forester drew out his knife and cut the ropes away from the boy and his father. They crouched for a minute close to the ground, unable to believe that they were free. Robin was about to urge them

to escape when another thought came into his head. Running round the clearing, he fired an arrow straight through the purse hanging from the Forester's belt.

"Now take the coins out of that fat purse you wear and give them to the boy."

As the Forester hesitated, Robin sent another arrow buzzing past him. Fumbling in his haste, the Forester emptied the coins from his purse into the boy's outstretched hand.

"Now go," Robin told the man and the boy.

"Master Outlaw," shouted the man, bowing towards the sound of Robin's voice. "I owe you my life. God bless you." And grasping his son's hand he ran into the shelter of the forest. Left alone, the Forester sat down on the ground. Wrapping his arms round his head, he began to moan and groan to himself.

Robin took one last look at the figure crouched beside the dead deer then set off at a loping pace for his father's house. He would have liked to have waited until the other Forester returned, but he knew that if he did he might be missed at home. There was a chance that they would examine the arrows, and, discovering that they were finely made, realise that they had not been fired by an outlawed peasant. It was just possible that they might come asking questions at Loxley Hall. It would be as well to have an alibi.

As Robin ran along the forest ways that he knew so well, he repeated in his mind the title that the man had given him – "Master Outlaw". He grinned and laughed aloud as he remembered the gibbering panic on the Forester's face. It had been a good morning. If only, thought Robin, life could always be like that, no tedious lessons, no endless sermons, then it would be worth living.

When he reached Loxley Hall he went in through the kitchens, climbing spiral stairs until he came to his old nurse, sitting sewing by a window high in the tower. She looked up at him, taking in his soiled hose and muddied boots, the tear in his sleeve and the half-empty quiver hanging from his shoulder.

"You have been running wild in the forest," she said, but only as a statement, not a reprimand. The days when it had been her task to try to control him were now past.

"No," Robin replied. "I have been with you all morning."

His dancing hazel eyes and wide, generous grin; his straight, tight body charmed her as they had always done. She shook her head ruefully, smiling against her better judgement.

"You have been with me all morning," she repeated obediently.

"He called me Master Outlaw," Robin told her.

"Who called you such names?" she demanded indignantly.

"It is a noble title," Robin replied, strutting in front of her. "When I take to the forest they will call me that."

"Tush on your nonsense. You, you will never be an outlaw. You will be a nobleman like your father."

"I have been with you all morning," Robin reminded her and was gone – light foot on the stone stairs.

He skimmed downwards until he came to a window that looked out over the ocean of green forest, the crests of the trees billowing like waves. Robin set his elbows on the windowsill. His knuckles bit into his chin as he stared out. Somewhere out there the Forester waited, thinking up tales of the band of violent outlaws who had attacked him and forced him to free his prisoners; somewhere the man and boy were free and had money to buy food for the sick woman.

"But if I had not been there . . ." Robin thought, shuddering as he pictured the starved faces of the man and boy and the tortures that would have been waiting for them. "And all for such a little thing! Shooting a deer when they run like rabbits in Sherwood. People starving while barons and bishops stuff their fat bellies." Robin snorted in disgust.

"If I were a peasant," he decided, "I should not stay scratching away at a wretched plot of ground and paying all my money to men I hated. I would take my family and live in the forest. A man could live well there." A shiver of excitement ran through him from head to toe. "But he should not have worn scarlet," Robin thought.

Then, speaking slowly, speaking aloud, so that his words were carried and lost over the green treetops of Sherwood, he said, "My men will never wear scarlet. They will wear russet in the autumn, drab for the winter, and for the bold days of spring and summer – Lincoln green."

Robin tipped back his head and laughed.

"Master Outlaw," he repeated. "Master Outlaw."

CHAPTER TWO

Robin Fitzooth stood outside the gates of Loxley Hall. He was a man now. The bow of yew he carried on his back was the full-sized bow of a grown man and his quiver was filled with broad clothyard arrows, flighted with goose feathers. He stood for minutes looking back the way he had just come, back at the home of his boyhood that was his no more.

Three years ago his father had died and Robin had inherited the estates of Loxley. Since he had become the Earl of Huntington, Robin had lived a wild and merry life. He could never resist a wager. More than anything he loved to set himself against another for a trial of strength, betting high sums on who could shoot the truest, ride the fastest or wrestle the most skilfully. Days of sport were followed by nights of feasting and the dead father's fortunes slipped through his son's fingers like air.

Two years after his father's death Robin had found himself in desperate need of money to pay off his debts. Much of his father's wealth had been invested in trading ventures and he knew that merchants would be returning from abroad, bringing him money.

"I will go to the monastery of St. Maries and ask to speak with the Abbot," he decided.

When the Abbot heard of Robin's plight he willingly agreed to lend him five hundred pounds on the condition that the money should be paid back to him in full within twelve months. If this was not done, all the lands of Loxley and the great Hall itself would belong to the Abbot.

Robin readily agreed to the bond, although he knew that the Loxley estates were worth far more than a mere five hundred pounds, worth at least ten times the amount of money he had borrowed from the Abbot.

"It does not matter," he told himself. "Long before next April Day I shall have money from my father's tradings. I shall pay the Abbot back in plenty of time."

But spring became summer, summer burnt into autumn and autumn turned to winter. Throughout the months, plenty of money came to Robin from his father's trading ventures, but each time the money was spent on other things. There was always a faster horse to be bought, a hound that he had to possess and wine to be laid in. Friends who needed a loan, or peasants who came to the doors of Loxley Hall, were never turned away.

It was not until the death month of February that young Robin gave real thought to his bond. His position was serious indeed. In six weeks it would be the first of April, April Day, and that day would bring the Abbot of St. Maries knocking at his doors and demanding his rights.

Even as March drew to a close Robin still refused to worry.

"There are many hours yet before I may expect the Abbot and in each of these hours many minutes. Each minute may bring a merchant riding up the drive to pay me my share of his profits," Robin told himself and tried to put the matter out of his mind.

But no merchant came.

When March ended, Robin had only managed to gather together a little over half of the money which he owed to the Abbot. When he had tried to sell his horses or his hounds what buyers there were had only offered low prices and it had seemed to Robin, who had no wish to sell his animals, that such poor prices were not worth accepting. Friends to whom he had lent money were still not able to repay him and all the poor folk who had received so much from Loxley Hall had fallen back into the landscape like last year's leaves.

16

"The Abbot is a holy man," he told himself. "He will not hold me to such an unjust bargain. I shall explain how matters stand and promise him full payment on the very day I receive money from my father's trading, or offer him land to cover the amount I cannot pay him. He is certain to accept that."

Late on the evening before April Day, a man in travel-stained clothing, mounted on a sweating horse, rode up to the doors of Loxley Hall and demanded to see the Earl of Huntington. A groom took his horse and a servant led him into the room where Robin was sprawled on a chair, uselessly brooding on tomorrow.

"Good sir," said the man, "I have come to speak with the Earl of Huntington."

"Speak on," said Robin.

"But I understand he is a man advanced in years."

"If you would speak with my father you must ride further than this earth allows," said Robin. "He died three years ago."

The man ducked his head in a quick gesture of sympathy.

"Then the news I bring will be for your ears."

"Aye," said Robin. "I am the Earl of Huntington now."

"I bring you word from Phillip of Ware. He sends sincere regrets that his trading ventures, in which your father invested some three hundred pounds, have been of such long duration. But I am here to tell you that his ship has now docked at Southampton and within three days you will receive your share of the monies."

"How much?" gasped Robin.

"Three times the amount your father invested . . ."

Robin's shouts of delight drowned the man's voice. Now he need no longer fear the Abbot's demands. The bond would be repaid in full in three days' time.

The Abbot came with the first light of April Day. He did not come alone. Twelve friars accompanied him, chosen not for their holiness but for their strength. Behind the friars were twelve armed men in the livery of the Sheriff of Nottingham, a close friend of the Abbot.

The Abbot sat in the great hall of Loxley and listened scornfully to Robin's explanations and excuses, and then commanded him to pay the bond money in full or to leave all his lands to the Abbot, as was clearly set down in the bond which he had signed.

"The bond date is this day. Have you the money?" demanded the Abbot.

"I have told you," cried Robin, beside himself with frustration and rage. "In three days I will have enough money to repay the bond in full."

"Our bond closes this day. Not in three days' time."

"In only three days I will repay it all."

"Can you pay your bond this day?"

"No, but . . ."

"Then by right of the justice of our land I claim all the lands of Loxley."

Seeing that the Abbot truly meant to have his estates, Robin sprang up from his seat and set his hand to his sword. For a second he paused, unwilling to draw arms on a Holy Father of the Church. In that second the Sheriff's men had him by arms and shoulders. Despite his struggles and protests they held him tightly while the Abbot read out the bond that had been agreed between them and formally took possession of Loxley Hall and all its lands. Then Robin was marched down the drive, thrust outside and the gates of his home were barred against him.

Robin sat down on a stone at the wayside. The sky was blue, the forest world about him shone green in the sunlight and the singing of the birds made the trees dance with life. He stared around and despite the hate which filled his heart against St. Maries' Abbot and the rage at his own feckleness, he could not truly feel anything except joy at being alive and young on such a morning.

"I have my bow and my health," Robin thought. "A

quiver full of right good arrows and a pair of well-soled boots upon my feet. I would be of poor spirit if I were to let such a louse as that Abbot spoil such a day for me." Then Robin remembered that on April Day the Sheriff of Nottingham was holding a shooting match in Nottingham. The prize was to be a butt of October brewed ale and it was to go to the man who shot the truest in the whole of Nottinghamshire.

"When we have drunk the barrel of ale dry I shall have made new friends and be in a better mind to regain my father's house and lands," Robin thought as he stood up. He took one last long look at the grey towers of Loxley Hall, then swung round and strode out on the road to Nottingham.

With each mile his heart grew lighter and his step more sure, for he knew that the butt of ale was his for the shooting. Young as he was, in the whole of Nottinghamshire there was no man who could shoot a straighter or a longer arrow than Robin of Loxley.

He had gone some eight miles when he came across a group of Foresters sitting by the wayside, eating and drinking. They were all dressed in the livery of the King and Robin would have passed them without a word, but the men called out to him, asking him where he was going and why.

Robin stopped, unslung his bow and, leaning on it, answered them squarely.

"I am on my way to Nottingham to shoot for the butt of ale and I dare say I shall win it."

"What, you young cock sparrow. You win it! When did the likes of you even have the right to draw a bow before the Sheriff? And what would you do with ale? Milk is your drink. Go back home to your mother," shouted one of the men.

At these words Robin felt the hot blood rise to his head, but not wanting to fight he tried to move on past the

19

Foresters, ignoring their jeers. Then one of the men sprang up and grabbed Robin by the shoulder, taunting him.

"Shoot," he cried, his breath stinking against Robin's face. "You have not yet the strength in those chicken bones to draw back the string of that bow you carry so proudly."

At the man's words Robin's temper raged like flame and he set an arrow to his bow.

"I'll wager you twenty marks," he swore, "that by the grace of Our Lady I shall take the buck from the deer who graze there."

The men, seeing the distance of the herd, roared with laughter.

"Young fool to think that you could attempt such a shot," mocked one.

"We'll take your wager," shouted another.

Robin's arrow sang straight and true and the buck sank down dead.

"Now," cried Robin, his heart high at his own skill, "pay me the money I have won."

The men had fallen silent and now stared sullenly at Robin.

"Get on with you," said the Forester who had caught Robin by the shoulder. "We had no wager with you. You are a marked man now, as dead as the King's deer you have just killed. Were your brains as good as your aim you should have known better than to have shot down a deer before the King's men. Think yourself lucky that we do not take you prisoner this minute."

Fury at being thwarted for the second time in one morning blazed like madness in Robin. He turned and walked grimly away from them, hearing their mockery buzzing like a swarm of bees behind him.

"Demented fool that I am," thought Robin furiously. "To lose my inheritance and to kill one of the King's deer . . ."

"Let this put feathers in your heels," yelled one of the Foresters, and as he spoke he set an arrow to his bow.

The shaft skimmed past Robin's ear and landed in the mud in front of him. Robin spun round. The arrow from his bow had reached the throat of the Forester almost before Robin knew what he was doing.

The Forester fell back, his life's blood spouting scarlet from his throat. His companions sprang to their feet, slipping bows from their shoulders, shouting with rage and astonishment. Some knelt to lift the dying man, some took aim at Robin, who was already vanishing into the cover of the forest.

All day Robin made his way deeper and deeper into the very heart of Sherwood. At first he followed the tracks and secret ways known to him all his life, but by evening he was approaching the depths of the forests where he had never dared to go before. He walked between giant oaks and beeches, their trunks as huge in the failing light as the mighty pillars of a cathedral. His hands and face were scarred and torn where, in his panic, he had pushed his way through the undergrowth of briar and hazel.

At last he stopped, standing still in the green strained light of the forest evening, his spirit heavy with the knowledge that he had killed a man. He knelt on the mould of the forest floor and prayed to Our Lady for forgiveness. Kneeling there, he took an oath upon himself that only in the most dire extremity would he ever again kill a fellow man.

It was on Robin's third day in the forest that he met up with three other outlaws – two men, one with a grizzled beard, the other with his ears cropped in punishment for some past crime, and a boy with a fox skin over his shoulders. They had lit a fire and were cooking meat. The smell of the food drew Robin to them. When he approached they jumped up, the grizzled man grasping a stout stave in his hand.

21

"Ho, stranger," he cried. "Make yourself known or you will feel my staff about your head."

Robin spread open his hands. "I am one of you, brothers," he said, knowing that his words were true. He was brother now to all the forest outlaws. Doubly outlawed, once for killing the King's deer and once for the murder of the Forester. If he were ever to be caught, his throat would wear the hangman's necklace and his feet would dance on air.

Robin was about to add his name when the earless man interrupted him.

"I think I know the cast of your face," he said. "When they cut my ears they were not too particular about the knife they used. My wounds would not heal and the suppuration entered my head. My wife, being told of a certain great house where she could obtain salves, went there and was given ointment that healed my head and a gold piece which saved my children from starving."

At the man's words Robin felt a sweetness stir in him. Since he had killed the Forester all had been black as midnight. It had seemed to him that all his life was cursed until the man brought back to him the memory of the poor who had come to Loxley for alms and had never been turned away. The memory seemed to Robin to be a gift from Our Lady and he swore in his heart always to be true to his vow.

"If I am right, and I am sure I am, do not give us your name," warned the earless man. "Cut-throats and thieves live in this forest. If there is a price on your head, many of them would be pleased to lay hands on the reward that would be theirs in exchange for your body. Forget your old name. Take a new one. Become a new man of Sherwood."

Robert of Loxley bowed his head to the man, knowing that he had been given good advice. "My name," he said, pausing, and into his head came the name his old nurse had used for him, "is Robin of the Wood."

"Nay," answered the grizzled man. "We are all of the wood. Let your name be Robin Hood. The hood you wear is rich enough to crown a king."

"Then Robin Hood I am," agreed Robin, shaking them all by the hand.

They sat together and shared the stew and when they had eaten they set up targets and shot against each other. Robin's skill outshone both men. When night came the boy was sent away and returned with skins of ale. The three, watched by the boy, drank and talked and lay back under the branches of the great forest trees.

"Will you join with us?" asked the grizzled man. "Your skill with the bow and our knowledge of the feast would go well together. Your arrows could find the heart of many a fat friar and our fingers pick gold from his saddle bags when he has no more need of it. We three could grow rich together."

Robin raised himself up on one elbow. "I have come into Sherwood," he said, "with an oath to Our Lady on my heart – to take no man's life; to rob only the rich so that their wealth may be given to the poor, and to gather round me men who think the same as myself so that in some way we may begin to put right the wrongs that afflict our land."

"That's moonshine talk," said the grizzled man. "Line your own purse first."

"Take gold where you can find it," agreed the other man. "The weaker the traveller, the less danger we will be in."

The home brewed ale had been strong and Robin rose unsteadily to his feet. "Then I must go my own way," he said. "For your companionship my thanks."

Robin Hood walked away from them into the forest.

He found a low. spreading oak, climbed into its branches, and eventually fell asleep.

When Robin woke in the morning, the boy with the fox's skin was curled at the root of the tree.

"I am your boy now," he replied when Robin questioned him. "What you said last night, that's what I feel. I do not want gold for myself. That is all those two ever think about. They do not care who they rob or kill. But I am for what you said; 'Rob the rich to feed the poor'. Let me stay with you?"

"And by my oath so you shall," cried Robin, grasping the boy's shoulders. "I shall call you Tod for the skin you wear. We shall be the first. They will come to join us, others who share our longing for justice. By our Lady, Tod, we will have a merry life in Sherwood."

CHAPTER THREE

So Robin Hood began his life in Sherwood. Soon no one remembered his old name or where he had come from, but many heard of his new name and came into the forest to find him and join his band. Some were men with a price on their heads for breaking the unjust laws of the forest, or for misdeeds against the Sheriff who, from Nottingham, governed the neighbouring area for the King. He was a man of power, having his own small army and caring little for any justice, being ruled only by his own greed. Some who came were peasants who could no longer endure their days of endless toil, the results of their labours being taken by the church in tithes, or by representatives of the King, in taxes. There were young gallants hot for adventure and true men, sick at heart to see the England they loved in the hands of Norman barons and to watch impotently while the Church, which should have succoured the poor, grew as greedy and as cruel as the nobles. These and many more sought out Robin Hood in order to join his band of outlaws.

Before they could join they all had to swear the great oath – to rob the rich and give to the poor, to withstand tyranny and to harm neither woman or child. When they had sworn, Robin would shake them by the hand, clasp them by the shoulder and welcome them to Sherwood. Each man was given a suit of Lincoln green for the summer months and one of drab brown for the winter. Each made for himself a bow of yew and arrows that flew straight and sure.

Although there were great feastings in the heart of Sherwood on the King's venison and ale brewed by the outlaws, there was also a great deal of work to be done – skins to be tanned, boots to be cobbled, clothes to be made, close watches to be kept so that no one moved in the forest without Robin knowing of it, and each day every man had to practise the skills of archery.

When Robin came among them at their practice he would set his arrows flying twice and three times the distance of their marks, with an aim so true that he could split a willow wand and then send his second arrow clean through the shaft of the first.

There was not one of the outlaws who did not worship Robin. They were awed by his skill with the bow and his wisdom of the forest ways. They loved his light step, his ready laughter and his bold heart that was always looking for new adventures. When they heard the sound of Robin's horn ringing through the forest, every man raced at full speed to answer the call, and there was not one of them who would not have given up his life to save his leader.

It was spring again. Robin Hood had lived in Sherwood for two years and had gathered about him close on a hundred men. Yet on this May morning Robin felt the need to go wandering on his own.

"Stay here," he said to the outlaws who were with him. "It is too long since an adventure came my way, and if it will not come to me then I must go and seek it out."

"Not alone," cried Will Stukley. "Take at least two other men with you. For the ransom on your head there's plenty of men who would gladly hand you to the Sheriff."

"I have my bow," replied Robin, "and at my belt my bugle horn. No man could travel more safely than I," and he strode on alone.

Robin came to one of the leys, long straight roads that cut through the forest, linking villages and leading to towns. Travellers passed him by and though Robin gave them all a fair good-day and a straight gaze from his twinkling eyes there was no sign of an adventure. No fat friar, his saddle bags clinking with coins taken from peasants and now being carried to a rich Abbot; no villager with a tale of injustice or a young girl needing his aid. After a time Robin turned away from the road and made his way towards the roofs of a village that was half hidden in the trees.

Close to the village ran a brook crossed by a long narrow plank which served as a bridge. As Robin approached the bridge, a man came striding towards it from the other side. When he saw Robin he quickened his pace so that he might cross first.

"By the saints," swore Robin. "What manner of man is this? More giant than man. The only place for such a man is in Sherwood with me."

Having paused in amazement at the sight of such a being, Robin ran swiftly to the bridge, unslinging his bow as he ran. Setting foot on the plank, he placed an arrow to his bowstring and faced the stranger.

The man advanced steadily to the centre of the bridge. He stood some seven feet high, was broad-shouldered as a bull, his legs like the trunks of oak trees, his massive arms swollen with muscle, and the vast hands that gripped his stout staff were as huge as haunches of prime venison. His black hair curled closely to his round skull and his dark eyes were fixed on Robin. At the centre of the bridge he stopped, set his staff before him and cried out his challenge.

"Loose that shaft from your bow and your head will ring like a church steeple a-jangle with bells from the kiss of my staff."

"Ass," cried Robin. "Long before your staff could reach me my arrow would have found your heart."

The giant leant forward on his stick. "You talk like the coward you are," he said. "A brave man who faces up so boldly to another carrying only a staff."

"I am no coward," cried Robin furiously. "Hold your place on the bridge while I cut myself a cudgel from the thicket and then I'll knock the word coward about your teeth.".

Robin laid his bow and arrows on the ground and cut himself a strong staff. The stranger watched, his lips curving into a smile as he flexed his muscles and stretched his great arms.

"Now," cried Robin, "whoever falls into the water first is the loser, the other has the victory."

"Agreed with all my heart," smiled the giant, and he set his staff to await Robin's onslaught as a man awaits the attack of a gadfly.

"Insolent fool," cried Robin and ran at the stranger. Their staves clashed, wood on wood, with the crash of red deer stags in the rutting season. Robin's bones were set jangling and even the giant felt the blow shatter through him.

"Take heed, little man," cried the stranger, raising his staff. "I shall crack your skull like a hazel nut."

Light footed, Robin danced before him. The staff crashed down but, ducking nimbly, Robin took only a glancing blow on the shoulder. Then he was through the giant's guard and set about his head with a fury of blows. The giant stumbled back, shaking his massive head like a stunned beast. Again Robin ran at him, but this time he was too slow and felt the giant's staff crack against his skull and blood trickle down his face.

Undaunted, Robin leapt backwards on the narrow plank as the giant surged forward. Robin feinted with his staff, ducked beneath the stranger's guard for a second time and closed in, his staff ringing about the head and shoulders of the giant. So fast and furious was the rain of blows that a sweat burst from the scarlet face of the stranger and rose in the air like steam.

Holding his staff by one end, the stranger fixed his eyes on Robin, let out a murderous roar and, charging at Robin,

dealt the outlaw such a batter upon the shoulders that he tipped him head over heels into the brook.

"Well, my bold bowman," laughed the giant as Robin surfaced, "where are you now?"

"Faith," spluttered Robin, "I am put to sea by your staff. The fight is yours. You are a sturdy villain and no mistake." Finding his feet, Robin waded to the bank and sprang back on to dry land. He shook himself like a dog, then, taking his horn from his belt, he set it to his lips and blew a blast on it that sounded deep into Sherwood.

From tanning and brewing, from shooting and cooking, the outlaws grabbed bows and full quivers and, like many parts of one body, they sped to answer their master's call. They burst through the trees and came running towards the brook.

"Why, you are wet to the skin," cried Will Stukley, staring in amazement at the state of his leader. "Did that rogue treat you so? Come men, we will give him a ducking that he won't forget." Some dozen of the outlaws grabbed the giant to force him into the water.

"No," cried Robin. "Set him free. He is a sturdy fighter and won by virtue of his strength in a fair bout."

As his men freed the stranger, Robin strode up to him, holding out his hand.

"Friend," he said, "my name is Robin Hood and these are my men, all good men and true. We live in the greenwood, harming no man save those whose fat needs the feel of our trimming knife. Come and join us. I need such a man as yourself to stand at my right side."

"Aye, that I will," cried the giant. "Many times I have thought of joining you to fight with you on the side of the poor folk. And having met you I like you the more. Yes, I shall join your band and fight right lustily for you." He grasped Robin's shoulder in his massive hand. "Robin Hood, I am your man."

Flames from the outlaws' fire leapt beneath the forest

boughs. The smell of venison wafted richly about the men who sprawled around the fire, ale pots at their sides.

Will Stukley rose to his feet. Advancing towards the great bulk of a man who sat by Robin Hood's side, he cried, "You have become one of us and yet you have still not given us your name."

"When this babe was born they gave him the name of John." The giant paused, a wide grin splitting his great face. "That is my name. John. John Little!"

On hearing his last name a roar of laughter rang out round the fire.

"Then take this for your new name," roared Will Stukley, tipping his mug of ale over John Little's head. "I stand god-father at this christening and name you Little John."

So the giant was known in Sherwood as Little John. He became the right hand man of Robin Hood, and of all the outlaws he was the closest to his master, staying with him to the hour of Robin's death.

CHAPTER FOUR

Two things remained with Robin from his old life – one was the ache in his heart for his true love, Marian Mortimer; the other was his desire to be revenged on the Abbot of St. Maries for his greed.

All Robin's men were charged to bring him word at once should the Abbot of St. Maries come near Sherwood. But the Abbot knew that Robin of Loxley had been outlawed and when tales reached him of a band of outlaws with their headquarters deep in Sherwood he reasoned that their leader, Robin Hood, might well be the young Robin of Loxley. So the Abbot, being of a shrewd and wary turn of mind, took pains to see that he kept well clear of the forest roads, and few things on earth would have persuaded him to enter Sherwood.

So it was that Robin had lived two years in the greenwood before his chance for revenge came to him.

The day was full summer, the trees heavy with leaf, the undergrowth a solid barrier of thorn and branch to those who did not know the forest. Robin was shooting at the marks, sending his arrows flying straight to their targets. Some thirty of his men stood around, watching their master's least breath. They were all skilled bowmen but never lost an opportunity to try to discover what it was in Robin that gave him such mastery with the bow.

Into the target ground ran Much the Millar's son. He paused for breath in front of Robin, his arms outstretched to proclaim the enormous news he carried.

"What tidings?" demanded Robin. "You come like a bull at a gate."

"Faster!" declared Much. "He has come. We have him at last."

Robin knew at once who he meant. "The Abbot of St. Maries?" he demanded.

"Along the west road with a hundred of the Sheriff's men, fifty marching before and fifty behind.

"One hundred men," cried Robin gleefully. "What a prize the Abbot must be carrying to need such an escort!"

Robin put his horn to his lips and set the greenwood ringing with three blasts, the call that would bring every outlaw straight to the great oak which grew at the very centre of their territory.

Robin swung himself into a low branch of the huge tree and laid one hand on its gnarled trunk as he gazed over the upturned faces of his men. Some were mere boys, some bearded as white as winter snows, and every age between, all sworn to right the wrongs committed by the nobles and clergy. Robin lifted up his hand for silence.

"Men," he cried, "the Abbot of St. Maries rides into our forest." He threw back his head and roared with delicious laughter. All the outlaws knew how Robin had been treated by the Abbot and an answering cry of delight broke from them.

"He comes with a hundred of the Sheriff's men to guard what he carries," continued Robin. "Shall we ask him to dine with us? What do you think?"

The outlaws' "Yes" came as if from one throat.

"He rides along the west road. If he is to accept our invitation we must persuade him to leave that broad road and take to a narrower path. That should not be difficult for a man of the Church, but knowing our Abbot he may require a little persuasion."

"Aye, then we shall give it to him," cried one of the men.

"George a Green, Wat Stummer, Grey Gos, Martin Lowe and Tod of the fox's skin, you shall all come with me,"

33

commanded Robin. "We shall bind up Wat's head and cover his face with deer's blood. Tod, we shall lay you on a litter as if you were dead. George, you will dress as a peasant, while Martin, Gray Gos and myself wear monks' robes. Together we shall come to meet the Abbot, making a great moan."

"All save me?" demanded Tod.

"Aye, you must be silent as the dead," chuckled Robin. "And we shall tell them how we were set upon by villainous outlaws who brought us to this sorry state before we could convince them that we knew nothing of the man they sought, a certain Abbot of St. Maries. Then, when their bowels are water, we shall offer to lead them along a safe way through the forest. We shall take them along the ride that leads by the five pines. You all know how it starts, a fine broad way that dwindles into a mere track."

"And over the track the branches of the trees meet like a roof," cried out Little John. "Five times a hundred men could lodge there unseen."

"Aye," agreed Robin, "and every man of you shall be hidden in those trees when I bring the Abbot beneath them."

Through the men went a shiver of anticipation.

"Little John, you shall lead the ambush. Choose your place with care. Do not go on until the track is too narrow or they may smell a rat."

Little John nodded, already planning the ambush.

"When I hear their approach," continued Robin, "I shall blow twice upon my horn so that you will be expecting us."

"It is well planned," shouted Much, and the outlaws roared their agreement.

"Good hunting, then," cheered Robin, swinging himself down from the oak.

"And a fat Abbot for our prize," echoed Little John.

In little more than five minutes the space around the

great oak where the outlaws had massed was completely empty. Only a few boys remained, preparing the feast for their expected guest.

At the side of the west road six men waited. The monk's hood was pulled well down over Robin's head, hiding his laughing eyes and ready grin which turned up the corners of his mouth at the thought of the next few hours' entertainment. Three other outlaws, also dressed in monks' robes, stood with him. One had his head swathed in blood-soaked bandages and his face encrusted with drying blood. The fifth man was wearing the clothes of a poor peasant, while Tod lay on a litter on the ground, invisible under the two cloaks that were covering him. Only his voice could be heard, demanding, a trifle shrilly, when he could get up for if he did not breathe fresh air soon, when they came to release him he would be truly dead.

"Silence, brat," said Wat, giving the hidden form a sound thumping as he spoke. "Do you wish to announce your presence to all who pass?"

"Soon there will be no one present to announce anything," muttered Tod rebelliously, rubbing his arm and making up his mind that should he ever return home he would never tell his family how he had been chosen to play a corpse while the rest of the band waited to fall upon their enemies.

"If I do not draw breath soon . . ." began Tod, but Robin's voice silenced him.

"Here they come," he announced and sent the notes of his horn ringing out into the forest.

The waiting outlaws heard it and climbed into the branches of the trees that arched over the track. They were completely hidden by the thick screen of summer leaves. Only a buzzard soaring high above them angled his head to focus more clearly on these strange new birds.

Minutes passed before the sound of marching feet could be heard clearly.

35

"Pick up the boy," said Robin. "And Wat, see that you groan your best. We must put on a pretty play for our Lord Abbot."

Robin led the way down the road to meet the Abbot. At his side came the battered monk, moaning in great distress and being supported by his brother monk. Behind them came the other monk and the peasant, carrying the litter on which Tod lay as still as if he were truly dead.

The marching men came into sight and in their midst, riding on mules, were the Abbot of St. Maries and four of his monks, each leading a pack ass that was heavily laden with panniers. From the panniers came the tell-tale clink of gold.

The Abbot clutched his reins and looked about anxiously. Every bird that flew from a tree made him flinch nervously and at the least sound he expected the forest blackness to become alive with bloodthirsty outlaws. Only the most dire necessity had forced the Abbot into Sherwood. The gold in his saddle bags was bound for the royal court as a gift to King Henry. The Abbot was to present the gold himself, at the same time mentioning in the most delicate fashion that should the King think fit to gift the lands of Merton to the Abbot, his gift would not be refused, nor would the Abbot be too concerned about the manner in which he knew the Lord of Merton, a brave Saxon gentleman, had met his death.

A jay burst chattering from the bushes and the Abbot's heart jumped into his throat with fear. He drew a linen handkerchief from his sleeve and mopped his brow. The friar riding alongside looked shrewdly at his superior.

"Mayhap," he suggested, "it would have been better for my Lord's peace of mind if we had taken the long road and not risked the dangers of Sherwood."

"And paid the Sheriff five more days' hire for his soldiers. Fie on your foolishness. We have nothing to fear from a common outlaw."

"No ordinary outlaw," said the monk, knowing well how the Abbot had come by Loxley Hall. "They say this Robin Hood would not be bettered by twice the men we have with us. They say . . ."

"Idle nonsense," cried the Abbot hotly, although his face was as white as a sheet. "I do not wish to hear that rogue's name mentioned in my hearing."

At that moment the men marching in front of the Abbot stopped, bringing the whole progress to a halt.

"By the rood," cried the Abbot, straining to see what had caused the halt, his nerves thrumming. "Get on," he shouted. "Get on with you." He urged his mount towards the head of the column.

At the sight of the bleeding monk and the body on the litter, the Abbot had to make a sudden grasp at his saddle as his head swam dizzily.

"Brothers, what has befallen you?" he gulped.

At this the injured monk groaned most horribly and leant even more heavily upon his companion.

"Outlaws and cut-throats," cried the leading monk. "Only a mile back along the road. They fell upon us like a pack of wolves, some two hundred or more."

The last drops of blood drained from the Abbot's face and his eyes stretched wide with fear.

"Before we could convince them that we were not the men whom they were seeking they had killed our lad and brought one of my brothers close to death, crying that they were the men of Robin Hood come to have their revenge."

"If it was not you, what men were they seeking?" whispered the Abbot through chattering teeth.

"Why a man of the Church, like ourselves," replied Robin, struggling to keep the laughter out of his voice and thankful for the monk's hood that hid his face. "One who had wronged their master."

"His name?" demanded the Abbot in terror.

"The name . . ." began Robin, pretending to have forgotten. He turned to the other monks. "What was the name they shouted?" he asked them and all the time his heart was light to see the Abbot's terror.

"Why, I have it now, it was – the Abbot of St. Maries."

On hearing his own name the Abbot of St. Maries swung dizzily in the saddle and would have swooned to the ground if two of the sheriff's men had not jumped to catch him.

"You were turned back by a mere outlaw," scoffed the captain.

"Near on two hundred," Robin corrected him. "Were I this Abbot I would not meet them with twice their number. They are mad for blood."

"Have you turned back?" gasped the Abbot, his fingers running like fat mice along his beads.

"Two of my brothers must take the boy for Christian burial," said Robin, "and brother Anthony must have his wounds dressed, but I am bound for London."

"Then you must face these brigands again?"

"In no manner," cried Robin, as if in fear. "My man is from these parts and knows of a way through the forest. We may take it safely since the outlaws wait a mile back for their victim. It will add three hours to my journey, but were it to add three days I would surely take it rather than face those fiends again." Robin waited, catching his breath to see if his carefully laid bait would be taken.

The Abbot hardly paused for a second.

"We shall come with you," he said, brushing aside the captain's protests. "We are most grateful for this warning. Come, let us make all speed to leave this wretched place."

"With your leave I shall walk ahead with my man," said Robin.

"As you will," stuttered the Abbot. "Only make haste."

Robin walked a little way behind George a Green as if he were following where he led. As the ride gradually grew narrower, Robin could hear the Sheriff's men grumbling amongst themselves. The soldiers had been unwilling to turn off the road instead of facing up to the outlaws, and as the track narrowed they began to look about suspiciously, saying to each other, "Who is this monk that leads us deeper into the forest?" One soldier who knew Sherwood well swore that he knew of no track that would take them through the forest.

"Oh, Little John," murmured Robin, "do not leave it too late." He glanced upwards, searching for signs of the outlaws.

Then, in the dense shadows of the forest boughs, he caught a glimpse of a bold, black eye that twinkled and winked and Robin knew that they were walking under the ambush.

With a great cry the outlaws dropped from the trees plum on to the men below. The Abbot cried like a whipped cur and his fear mixed with the cries of rage as the soldiers, taken completely by surprise, struggled to draw their weapons.

The fight was violent but short-lived and in no time the Sheriff's men were completely overpowered. Their hands lashed together, arrows pointing at their throats, they stood watching helplessly as Robin Hood, having thrown off his monk's robes, stood before the Abbot clad in Lincoln green, his longbow in his hand.

"How now, my good Lord Abbot," Robin cried. "A thousand welcomes to my new estates."

The Abbot's face was the colour of old porridge and the huddle of monks standing beside him shook visibly.

"When last we met you were so fond of me that you moved into my house uninvited, but now set your mind at ease, for here you are invited and to a right good feasting. You will see that my lands are somewhat broader than when I dwelt in Loxley, so come, make free here as you did before, and if you wish to stay, why, you will be most welcome." A peal of laughter echoed through the trees.

Some of the outlaws stayed to guard the soldiers while

the rest went with Robin and led the blindfolded Abbot and his monks through Sherwood until they came to the clearing by the vast oak, where they dismounted.

"Come, be seated," commanded Robin, guiding the Abbot to his own oak tree chair and taking off his blindfold while the other monks were seated on logs. The rest of the outlaw band made themselves comfortable on the ground, and wooden platters were passed around and swiftly filled with thick slices of venison and pickled vegetables. Great jugs of ale were set within the reach of every man and the lads of the outlaw band, including Tod, slipped busily to and fro, refilling them as the men drank down the strong beer.

"You are not eating," laughed Robin, looking down scornfully at the Abbot's shaking hands. "Is our fare not good enough for you?"

"I am not hungry," mouthed the Abbot.

"You had appetite enough on our last meeting," Robin reminded him. "So fair an appetite that in one gulp you ate up my lands and house, horses and hounds and all my means."

"It was in the bond," whimpered the Abbot. "It was mine by law."

"An eighth of my land would have more than met the bond," snarled Robin and for a second it came back to him how this man, now in his power, had taken from him all that he once owned. "I was a green boy then and you were so swinish in your holy greed that you would not wait three days but took all that I had. You ate then of your own accord so I say that you shall eat now, whether you would or no."

The Abbot felt the prick of Little John's dagger set against the fat at his waist.

"Eat!"

With shaking hands the Abbot pushed the greasy slices of meat into his mouth, chewing at it, trying desperately to swallow it, for his throat was clenched with fear and he expected every moment to be his last.

"Drink," ordered Robin, passing him a tankard filled with water. "If this ale is thinner than you are used to, think on the wine you took from my father's cellars."

The Abbot sipped at the water with trembling lips.

"Faster," cried Little John, and snatching the tankard from him, poured it over his head.

While the others were feasting, six of the band had counted out the money in the little asses' panniers and when they had finished they brought the panniers and laid them at Robin's feet.

"Three thousand pounds," they told him.

"So little," cried Robin, starting up in mock dismay. "Why, my Lord Abbot, that will not pay for all you have eaten. We must take it all and ask for more."

"Rogue and scoundrel," spluttered the Abbot, but the prick of Little John's dagger stopped his words. "I have no more."

"Why then," mocked Robin, "if you speak true you must pay in some other manner. You shall preach us a sermon, for we are all poor sinners in need of your Lordship's guidance. Stand up, my Lord, and preach to us."

The outlaws, hearing Robin Hood's words, crowded around, adding their cheers to Robin's encouragement, but the Abbot's legs were water and he could not stand.

"He lacks a pulpit," cried Will Stukley. "Let us tie him to the oak, that will put words into him."

Although they tied the Abbot to the tree, still he could find no words.

"Then," said Robin, "repeat for us the tenth of Our Lord's commandments, telling us how we shall not covet our neighbour's goods."

But even this was too much for the exhausted Abbot. His mouth clapped open and shut but he could make no sound.

"Cut him free," ordered Robin at last. "Since we have an Abbot who cannot preach we shall make him dance for his supper. Dance, my Lord Abbot, dance as you once danced your way into my lands."

From foot to foot the terrified Abbot hopped.

"Faster," cried Robin and sent an arrow into the ground at the Abbot's feet. "Ha, ha, you have ginger in those toes that we have not seen yet." He shot again at the jogging Abbot.

This way and that he hopped and skipped, a desperate, pathetic figure; his eyes wide with terror, his arms loose as a puppet's, his feet flapping hecticly as he danced to the music of the outlaws' arrows.

"Enough, enough," cried Robin at last, wiping the tears of laughter from his eyes as the Abbot collapsed, moaning, to the ground. "You have made good a little of your debt with such a merry jig, and what you have still to pay will keep until we meet again. Away with you."

Little John brought up the Abbot's mule and three of the outlaws hoisted him into the saddle.

"He is sitting the wrong way round," cried out one of the men.

"Why, so he is," agreed Little John. "He is facing the beast's head." Girding the Abbot's waist with one of his giant arms, Little John plucked him from the saddle and sat him down facing the mule's tail.

So it was, facing his mule's rump, that the Abbot of St. Maries was led back to join the Sheriff's soldiers.

That night when Robin Hood lay on his bed of bracken and deerskin he laughed aloud for sheer delight at the memory of the day that was past. Not one coin of the Abbot's money did he keep for himself. Some went into the outlaws' coffers, the rest was given to the poor. Even as Robin lay under the stars his men walked through the villages, leaving a gold coin in doorways or on windowsills, wherever the outlaws knew of a peasant in need.

"By my soul, how he did dance," thought Robin and laughed until the tears sprang to his eyes.

But there was no laughter in the great hall of Nottingham Castle. The Sheriff of Nottingham, that man of power and arrogance, sat late into the night, talking with his friend the Abbot of St. Maries.

"We shall not tolerate it one day more," swore the Sheriff, crashing his fist down on the great elm table. "I shall ride to London myself to tell King Henry how our lives are made intolerable by this arrant knave."

CHAPTER FIVE

The Sheriff of Nottingham stood before King Henry in the courtroom of the Palace of Westminster. Around them the courtiers' gowns were bright as a July flower border and from the stone walls hung banners and richly-woven tapestries. Light from the flaring torches made the jewelled rings on King Henry's fingers dusk and glint as he twisted his hands impatiently. His brows were drawn together and his mouth set in a hard, ill-tempered line as the Sheriff's voice droned on, relating tale after tale of Robin Hood's misdeeds. But at the King's side Queen Eleanor leant forward, listening intently to the Sheriff's tales of the bold outlaw's daring.

The Sheriff told the King how the outlaws lived off the King's own deer and were so secure in the heart of Sherwood that no Forester dare go near them; were so full of guile that no honest man dare take the roads by the forest for fear of their arrows, and how the peasants who received gifts from the outlaws were beginning to question the rights of the barons and the teachings of the Church.

"Why, only last month this rebellious rogue waylaid the good Abbot of St. Maries and took from him three thousand pounds that was being brought by the Abbot as a gift to your Majesty. And right scurrilously did that wretch treat the Abbot, forcing him to eat your Grace's venison and to dance frivolously, and tying him upon his mule face to tail."

Queen Eleanor smothered a laugh but the King's patience had reached its limit.

"Too much," he roared and his words set the nobles stirring and quivering uneasily as if a wind blew through the

44

flower border, for they all knew and dreaded the wrath of the King.

"Stuff your great foot into your prattling mouth. Do you come here to have the noose fitted about your own scrawny neck, that you come snivelling before me, accusing yourself? Or is it the kiss of my executioner's axe that you seek?"

"Nay, my Lord," cried the Sheriff in dismay, his little eyes popping from his head, his pink, moist lips sucked in with shock. "Nay, not so." The Sheriff dropped to one knee in front of the King. "I seek your royal aid to help me overcome this bandit and his outlaws."

The King stretched out his foot and with a violent kick sent the Sheriff sprawling on to the floor.

The courtiers drew back, their robes folded close into their bodies against the coming storm. Even the Queen, although her blue eyes were still bright at the tales of Robin Hood's daring, gripped the arms of her throne, her knuckles gleaming like pearls through her transparent skin.

"Lives in my forest! Dines off my venison! Takes three thousand pounds meant for me! Mocks the rule of the Church!" cried King Henry. "While you do nothing but come whining like a cur dog, snivelling at my feet. Are you not my Sheriff? Are you not appointed to keep the rule of the King in Nottingham and Sherwood?"

"But . . . but . . ." began the Sheriff, struggling to his feet.

"Get you gone," roared the King, "and root out this rogue who flaunts our laws. Carry out the duties to which you are appointed or your head will add a new bauble to the walls of Nottingham Castle."

The Sheriff rode back to Nottingham in high dudgeon, his sour blood boiling at the treatment he had received from the King. He knew that the men who were riding escort beside him had heard how he had been received by the King and his mind shrivelled away from the thought of their tales being spread throughout Nottingham, growing taller with each retelling.

When the Sheriff reached Nottingham he set about organising the capture of Robin Hood. He increased the price on Robin's head, but only a few went into the forest thinking to bring back the outlaw's body. Some who did turned and fled when they discovered how the dense forest could whisper and laugh about them, and how the green cushion of moss at their feet could suddenly sprout a quivering arrow when nothing else in the forest had moved and their fearful eyes could see no sign of the bowman who had fired.

Some of the stouter-hearted who went on into the forest were taken by Robin's men and brought before their master. They were feasted on venison and ale, given a display of breath-taking archery, fell under Robin's spell and became members of his band. But most men, hearing of the new reward, only smiled and passed by, remembering the gold coins that had appeared as if by magic to save children from starvation or to buy grain or cattle.

When the increased reward brought no results, the Sheriff mustered his troops and on a morning in July rode into Sherwood with two hundred men. A month later he rode out again, and in the whole month he had seen nothing more of the outlaw band than their arrows whistling through the trees. Sherwood was a village to the outlaws, but to the soldiers it was a place of terror where every step might lead them into a swamp or an ambush, where every crackling twig might mean death from an outlaw's arrow.

"Then you have not captured him?" asked Sir Hugh of Flamyards when he sat drinking with the Sheriff of Nottingham. "And how long did you spend in Sherwood?"

"A month," admitted the Sheriff sullenly, and crashing down his goblet he sprang to his feet and began to stride up and down, his mouth working furiously, his beady eyes starting from his head with rage.

"That upstart of a louse," he swore. "I shall slit him from gizzard to gutch. He will see his own guts spilling over his feet before he dies."

"But first," reminded Sir Hugh gently, "the capture."

"Take care who you mock," threatened the Sheriff, throwing himself back into his chair and gesturing to his page to refill his goblet. "I shall capture him and all who follow him."

"Oh, I doubt it not," soothed Sir Hugh. "But how? Do you plan to start a winter campaign? If you cannot master Sherwood in the summer, you will not survive the winter. Nor would his Majesty be pleased to wait so long for news of the outlaw's capture."

The Sheriff grunted, tipped back his goblet, drinking noisily, and held it out again to be refilled. As the page poured out the wine a few drops spilt on the Sheriff's sleeve.

"Dolt," he cried, hitting the boy soundly about the head. "Son of a cow." He moved his goblet away too quickly, again causing the page to spill the wine and merit another clouting.

"Then tell me," the Sheriff demanded, thrusting his head out at Sir Hugh, "seeing you know so much, how would you take this Robin Hood?"

"Being a fat man, I would sit here and wait for him to come to me."

"You would invite him to stay?" sneered the Sheriff.

"I would lure him," corrected Sir Hugh, smiling slowly. "I would hold . . . " He paused as if savouring the idea upon his tongue. "I would hold an archery competition, as you have done before, and I would make the prize so valuable that no man who could draw a bow would be able to resist entering. They would come, all clad in Lincoln green, running into your trap. You would have no trouble awarding the prize, no trouble recognising this Robin Hood."

The Sheriff's face shone like an October full moon.

"The prize of a golden arrow," he crowed. "That would bring them out of their hiding place."

The evil laughter of the two men echoed in the pageboy's ears as he stood silently behind the Sheriff, listening to their plans to capture Robin Hood.

Will Stukley brought news of the contest to the outlaws.

"All bowmen are challenged to the match and the prize is to be an arrow of pure gold."

"When is this contest?" Robin demanded.

"A week come Saturday," said Will. "In the courtyard of Nottingham Castle. The arrow to be presented by the Sheriff himself."

"Why," cried Robin in mock alarm, "that is too soon. I shall not have enough time to prepare."

"Time or not," warned David of Doncaster above the laughter of the men, "you must not take such a risk. Were the Sheriff to see you, why, your next resting-place would be Nottingham jail."

"What would you have me do?" demanded Robin, turning on the young man. "Sit here sucking my thumbs while the Sheriff presents the prize to another?"

But many of the outlaws agreed with David of Doncaster.

"You know well how he has tried to track you down," cautioned George a Green. "Would you walk into his grasp?"

The frown on Robin's face deepened. He opened his mouth to tell his men that he had not known that they were such timid rabbits when there was a sound of running footsteps coming towards them through the trees. The outlaws who were on guard fitted arrows to their bows while the rest of the men stood ready to spring into action.

Through the trees came Tod, grasping another boy of

about his own age tightly by the hand. Both boys were scarlet in the face and breathless.

"Master," cried Tod, halting in front of Robin. "I bring you news of great danger."

"Not another come to tie me back to my mother's apron strings," joked Robin, then seeing the hurt expression on Tod's face he bit back his laughter. "Tell us this news."

Tod dragged his companion forward. "Speak," he commanded. "Tell Robin Hood what you told me when I found you."

The boy looked up at Robin. His rich clothes were torn and spoiled, his fine leather shoes ruined; his face was filthy and beaded with dried blood where thorns and brambles had scratched him, his fair hair, cut in the straight fringe of a pageboy, was matted, but his blue eyes looked up fearlessly at his hero, Robin Hood.

"I was the page of the Sheriff of Nottingham," the lad announced in a clear voice, ignoring the gasps of surprise which greeted his words. "But I am no longer in his service. I have come to serve you and to live the free life of the greenwood."

"Your news," urged Tod in a breathless whisper. "Tell them your news. What you heard."

"The shooting match for the golden arrow is not a true contest. While I was serving the Sheriff I heard him plan it all. It is a trap. He is only holding the contest to lure you to Nottingham. If you go, as he is sure you will, you will be taken prisoner. All his men have orders to scrutinize each archer before he is allowed to shoot and when they recognize you or any of your men they will arrest you."

The outlaws who had already warned Robin not to go to Nottingham redoubled their warnings, and even the boldest men were silent, thinking it would be a foolhardy venture and no golden arrow worth the risk. But Robin set his hands on his hips and laughed at them all.

"A pox on your fears. I shall pluck this arrow from between the Sheriff's teeth."

"And the same teeth will close about your neck," stated Will Stukley.

But Little John, seeing that his master was set on the venture and having a liking in his own heart for such a jest, described a plan which would allow Robin to compete for the arrow and remain unrecognised.

The sun blazed down from a cloudless sky. In the tiers of seating overlooking the targets set up for the archery contest the noblemen and gentry of Nottingham sat dressed in silks, satins and velvets. The Sheriff, in his ermine-trimmed robes, sweated freely but he paid no attention to the heat. He leant forward, staring down at the crowds beneath him, gnawing at the knuckles of his clenched fists.

The common people were kept back from the marks by ropes slung between poles. Many had brought food with them and they sat on the grass, eating and drinking. Some were laying wagers on a favourite bowman, others telling tales of past contests, all anxious for the shooting to begin.

Separated from the crowds, the archers waited, testing bowstrings, taking practice aim. They were dressed more brightly than the people, many wearing the livery of their masters.

By the Sheriff's side sat Sir Hugh of Flamyards. His huge belly was resplendently draped in maroon velvet, his grey beard skilfully trimmed and tinted blue.

"Well, do you see them?" demanded the Sheriff. "For I see no trace of them. Not a thread of Lincoln green."

Sir Hugh yawned, although it had been his idea, he felt none of the Sheriff's urgency.

"The wretch has not had the courage to leave his bolt hole. He skulks in the protection of Sherwood," ranted the Sheriff, thinking of the cost of the golden arrow.

"More than likely," agreed Sir Hugh, stifling another yawn. "Is it not time for the contest to begin?"

When the Sheriff did at last give the order to allow the shooting to commence there were still no archers in Lincoln green waiting to shoot for the golden arrow, nor any who resembled any of the outlaws.

"Search each face well," the Sheriff warned his captain.

"They could not pass our scrutiny," the captain assured him. "Should any of those rogues dare to come here today they'll never leave again."

As each archer stepped forward to shoot, the Sheriff's men asked his name and where he came from, and while the man answered they looked carefully at his features and dress.

The crowd knew many of the archers. They cheered their favourites and jeered at those they disliked but were always ready to encourage a brave shot even if the archer was a stranger.

"I think nothing of that one," stated a loud-voiced woman from the crowd, as a beggar, dressed in dirty rags, who was almost the last to shoot, stepped forward. "He were better to use his arrows to hold his rags together."

The beggar limped towards the Sheriff's men. One gripped him by the shoulder and hurried him forward. Stumbling, the beggar just managed to stop himself from falling.

"Your name?"

"Jack. I have no other."

"Then, Jack, stir yourself to shoot before the devil collects his own."

As the beggar set up his longbow and took aim, the Sheriff's men watched complacently.

"Even the bold Robin Hood, who they say turns none away, would not accept that bundle of tatters," said one. Laughing, the others agreed with him.

51

But the beggar's arrow sang sweetly from his bow and buried itself into the target closer to the centre than any other arrow that had been shot before. The Sheriff's men had no choice except to signal to the beggar to join the twelve archers whose arrows had also hit the inner ring of the target.

When all had shot there were still only thirteen archers to shoot again in the second round of the contest. This time they stood further back from the target and only five survived. Included in these five was the beggar.

Again the five shot from a greater distance, and only two hit the centre ring. These two were Sam a the Mill, one of the most skilled bowmen in the district, and the other was the beggar, still stumbling and staggering and clutching at his dirty rags.

This time they stood back the full length from the target. The crowd, who knew the mean dealings of Sam a the Mill, were all cheering the unknown beggar and many of the ladies clapped their dainty hands and vowed that if the beggar was not so old and so filthy he would be a fair yeoman. But one of the ladies sat very still, her brown eyes fixed on every move the beggar made. Her name was Marian Mortimer and although she was slender, with a light step and a good humour, she was still unwed. Two years ago she had seen the last of her true love, Robin of Loxley when he had been outlawed. Marian believed that he lived now in Sherwood, using the name of Robin Hood, and often she would dream of joining him there. She had never looked at another man, yet today there was something about the beggar who was shooting so boldly that made her heart lift and brought colour to her cheeks.

Sam a the Mill was to shoot first.

The Sheriff watched sullenly. This should have been his moment of triumph for he had been certain that Robin Hood would win the arrow. The Sheriff had rehearsed the moment over and over again in his mind. How, as he presented the golden arrow to Robin Hood, his men would surround him and Robin would be in his power at last.

Sam a the Mill took careful aim, checking his stance, the direction of the breeze, and making a great show of his own skill. His arrow flew true, coming so close to the very centre of the target that the crowd groaned, certain that Sam must have won.

Stumbling, fumbling, almost tripping over his own bow, the beggar took his stand. He set his arrow to the bowstring as if he knew little of the art, then, with hardly a glance at the target, he drew back his bowstring and as if by itself the arrow took flight.

A gasp rose from the crowd and turned into a roaring cheer, for the beggar's arrow lay buried in the target closer to the centre than the arrow which was already there – so close that from a distance they looked like one arrow, but the beggar's arrow lay on the inside and was at the very centre of the target.

With bad grace the Sheriff presented the golden arrow to the beggar. Sir Guy, sensing his friend's ill-controlled rage, had left before the presentation.

"I had meant this for a better than you," the Sheriff told the beggar. "But he was too lily-livered to accept my challenge. He skulks like the coward he is, afraid to leave the safety of his forest."

For a moment the beggar looked directly at the Sheriff, his hazel eyes alight with scorn and contempt, then he took the arrow, and buried it in his ragged clothing. Marian, who was still watching the beggar thought for a wild instant that it really was her lost love. For a split second the beggar looked straight at her. Their eyes met and Marian knew that it was Robin of Loxley in disguise. His name formed on her lips, but before she could speak he had turned away and was lost in the throng.

"It was Robin," she told herself. "And he knew me.

But he thinks of me only as a weak, silly girl who would be a burden round his neck."

"What ails you?" asked her mother sharply. "Has the sun touched you too strongly?"

But Marian hardly heard her for the sudden resolve that had formed in her mind, the resolve to learn to shoot an arrow as truly as Robin himself and to handle a sword as well as any man. Then she would be a fit mate for Robin Hood.

As Robin jostled his way through the crowds he saw nothing but the vision in his mind's eye of Marian – her auburn curls, her gentle brown eyes and her slim grace. "She could not possibly have recognised me," he lied to himself. "Never could I take her from her family and home or ask her to endure the hardships of life in Sherwood. I have no right even to think of her. She would not marry an outlaw." Resolutely Robin barred all thoughts of Marian from his mind. Yet still his heart whispered her name.

Later that night the golden arrow hung from a single thread, spinning like a weather vane from a branch of the great oak at the heart of Sherwood. Robin sat at the foot of the oak, ale jug in hand, the rags of his disguise flung behind him, still jubilant from his success.

"Not one soul there saw through my disguise," he crowed, staring up at the glinting arrow. "Yet one thing vexes me. I like it little that the Sheriff should think me a coward."

"That is easily put to rights," said Little John. "Tomorrow he will think that no longer."

The next day when the Sheriff rode to worship, an arrow buried itself into the leather of his horse's saddle. His men drew their swords but there was no sign of anyone who could have fired it.

"There is a message on it," said the soldier who had plucked the arrow from the saddle.

The Sheriff snatched the piece of paper that was pierced on the arrow, but not before the soldier had had time to read it.

"*Yon beggar was none but bold Robin Hood, and your arrow hangs now from his oak in Sherwood,*" read the Sheriff.

At a high window Little John was filled with silent laughter to see the Sheriff's rage. The soldier who had read the message could hardly wait to tell his friends, and by that evening the whole of Nottingham knew how Robin Hood had tricked the Sheriff in his own city.

CHAPTER SIX

Autumn burnished the forest to red gold. Early frosts rimed the grasses and rusted the bracken. The air was sharp and the sky silver blue. In a clearing, some three dozen of Robin's men were practising their skills with the broadsword. The wine of the bright morning sharpened their senses, sent their blood racing as they thrust and parried, fighting over the carpet of crisp leaves, the crash of their weapons booming through the trees.

Gradually each pair of opponents called a truce and fell back to the edge of the clearing to watch the remaining men, until only one pair was left. One man of the pair was tall and lithe, the other an oak tree in motion – Robin Hood and Little John. Since their first meeting on the plank, the two had crossed swords and staves many times and each knew all the tricks of the other.

They moved, now fast, now slow, giving and receiving blows of such power that they would have dropped any other man to the ground. Little John's blade struck down upon his master's left shoulder, crashing against the chainmail he was wearing for protection. Robin side-stepped, letting the sword blade slide down his back while, with both hands on the hilt of his sword, he hit Little John a punishing blow beneath his right arm, crashing into the giant's armour.

A cheer rose from the watching men, and the bright-eyed lads, sitting like squirrels in the branches of the trees, could not speak for excitement.

Little John swung his blade in a great circle about himself, whistling the air, but Robin had ducked, twisted round, and come at Little John again, quick-footed as a boy, with a powerful blow to his head with the flat of his blade. The blow sent Little John stumbling forward, his foot caught on a root and he crashed to the ground like felled timber.

Robin swung his sword this way and that, in glinting patterns of triumph while the lads in the trees screamed as shrill as gulls.

"Enough, enough," cried Robin as Little John struggled to his feet and made at Robin again. "We will fight another time, and next time, as like as not, your brawn will beat my brain!"

Little John took off the metal cap that had been protecting his skull and eased his body inside his chain-mail vest.

"When I have starved for a winter I shall be more fit to follow your dance," he said. "As for some of us who have little on their bones by this fat autumn they may be singing a different tune before they see the spring."

"Who knows," agreed Robin. "Yet what I do know is that were I to take the fastest horse in all Nottinghamshire and ride ten days in any direction I would not find a better swordsman than yourself, Little John."

"Not so," said Will Stukley. "Only ten miles from this very spot there lives a swordsman second to none. He would make mincemeat of Little John and I would not lay a wager between yourself and this man."

"What name has this fellow?" cried Robin.

"He is the curtail friar of Fountainhead Abbey, or Friar Tuck, as he is known."

At first when Little John had heard Will Stukley's words his face had bloomed scarlet with rage, but when he heard who it was that Will Stukley meant his expression mellowed, and his eyes flickered with memories.

"Aye," said Little John. "I have met the man. He did not make mincemeat of me, though if any should manage it he would be the one." Little John chuckled at memories from the past.

Robin's curiosity burned like flame in dry tinder. "Tell me more of this wonder man?" he demanded. "Is he a monk that he dwells at Fountainhead?"

"Once he was," said Will Stukley. "But the Abbey could not contain such a one. He lives in a small stone dwelling outside the walls of Fountainhead, ever ready to give a blessing or a shriving. And being himself no small part of Mother Church, he rightly uses the alms people pay him to support himself. Should there be no offering and the passer-by rich, why, Tuck's sword will slit their money bags and send their coins jingling into his hands."

"Such a one," cried Robin, "speaks to my heart. He should not be left to waste there. His place is here in Sherwood at our side."

"He will not come unless he wishes so of his own free will," warned Little John.

"We shall see how my sword can shape his will," said Robin, already setting his metal cap back on his head and pulling his hood over it, then covering his chain-mail with his jacket of Lincoln green. "I shall search out this Friar Tuck."

Will Stukley led the way to Fountainhead Abbey. Little John, curious to see his old rival again, and four more of the outlaws looking for a day's adventure, came with them.

"There," said Will Stukley at length, when the forest path they had been following opened out to green pastures that sloped down to a fast-flowing river. "There is Fountainhead." He pointed across the river to where the roofs of the Abbey could be seen through the trees.

"We will find Friar Tuck somewhere about here," declared Little John, and would have gone bounding down to the river if Robin had not called him back.

"Wait here," Robin told his men. "I have a mind to meet this famous friar by myself."

"Take your wits with you," warned Will Stukley. "He is a cunning rogue."

"I have my horn," said Robin. "One blast will bring six brave men to aid my wits," and he walked on alone.

The outlaws turned back into the trees and stretched themselves out under the warmth of an autumn sun.

"We had best keep an ear open for the sound of his horn," Little John observed as he passed round the skin of ale that he had carried at his belt. "If I know that Tuck I think we shall be hearing our master's call before long."

Robin followed the rolling, peat-brown river, searching for a bridge or a ford where he might cross. His heart was light within him at the thought of finding a man to join his band such as this Friar Tuck promised to be.

Soon Robin reached a place where the river flowed more slowly. He took a stick, and, testing the depth of the water, knew that it would reach over his thighs if he waded across. Having no wish for such a wetting, Robin looked around but could see no other way of crossing. It seemed if he was to find Friar Tuck he must risk a soaking.

Reluctantly Robin paused before stepping into the water, and at that moment he saw a figure sitting on the opposite bank. He was half hidden by a knot of willow trees but Robin could see that he wore a friar's habit. His head was tonsured with a shaved crown and a halo of black curls. His face was round as a whole cheese, round as the pie which he was cramming into the huge cavern of his mouth. Beneath his friar's robes, which were kirtled into the cord at his waist, two solid legs planted enormous bare feet into the soft earth at the riverside, and the hand that felt for the second pie to follow the first down his gaping maw cast a thunderous shadow over the ground.

"Why," thought Robin, "here's a sturdy horse to take me across the river." Fitting an arrow to the string of his bow he aimed it straight at the heart of the fat friar.

"Brother friar," he called. "Do you wait there to act as a ferryman? For I would cross your river and as you have no boat that I can see, I needs must ride upon your back."

At first Robin thought that the man had not heard him for he gave no sign that he was aware of a stranger. Slowly and deliberately he packed the last piece of pie into his mouth, dusted the crumbs off his lips and slowly wiped his hands on the hem of his gown.

Robin was about to challenge him a second time when the friar stood up and faced him. His eyes peered out of his fat face like twin currants stuck into risen dough, but they regarded Robin shrewdly enough.

"Since I wear the medal of our blessed Saint Christopher you may put down your bow. I shall come for you and carry you across."

With these words the friar belted up his gown, buckled on a broadsword that even Little John would have been hard pressed to wield, set his steel cap upon his shaven head and strode into the river. The flowing waters split before him as if an island were on the march. When he reached the opposite bank he bent his broad back and without a word Robin climbed on to his shoulders, and, sitting high and dry, was carried to the other side.

On the far bank the friar deposited Robin on the ground and quick as a wink had drawn his sword and held it over Robin's head.

"Now," cried the friar, "let me see you return my Christian charity. It would please me to be carried to the other side." When Robin opened his mouth to object he felt the stab of the friar's sword.

"Step fair," commanded the friar, balancing himself on Robin's shoulders like a fully-blown blossom on a slender stem.

The friar was some three times the weight of Robin, nor did Robin's feet know the crossing as the friar's had done. Each time Robin hesitated or stumbled, the friar dug his heels into his sides or tweaked his ears to guide him to left or right.

"If Little John could see me now," Robin thought. "This fat friar has made a fool of me."

This time, when they reached the bank, Robin Hood was the faster. He pretended to stumble, lobbed his rider on to the bank, and in one sure spring was kneeling beside him, his dagger tickling the friar's fat chins.

"Since we are now back where I started from, we shall need to begin again and this time it is my turn to ride."

Never a word said the friar, even when Robin, thinking on how he had been treated, began to beat his fat behind with the flat of of his sword, urging him to greater speed.

It was not until they had reached the middle of the river that the friar lowered his head, bunched his shoulders and, giving a mighty heave, chucked Robin head first into the water.

Before Robin, spluttering and gasping, had found his feet, the friar was on dry land, drawing his sword.

Standing thigh deep in the swirling water, Robin sent arrow after arrow against the fat bulk of the friar, but the friar's steel buckler protected him and turned Robin's arrows as if they had been twigs.

"Shoot on," mocked the friar, "and when all your arrows are spent, come out and fight like a man."

Robin shot all his arrows, thinking to hit the friar in an unprotected part, but the friar, for all his bulk, moved as nimbly as a cat, and not a scratch had he received when Robin was at last forced to climb up the bank, drawing his sword. The two men charged at each other with the clash of steel on steel.

At first Robin fought blindly, so furious was he at all the humiliations which had been heaped upon him. There was not one of the outlaws who could have withstood the fury of Robin's sword when his blood surged high with fury. Even Little John could not have stood against the range and thrust of Robin's blows as he lunged and parried on spring-heeled feet. But the friar was agile and quick-

witted and drove his sword blows with the charge of a full-grown bull behind them, easily containing Robin's whirlwind attack.

Gradually Robin's temper cooled and he began to fight with his usual skill and tactics, yet so evenly matched were the two men that they fought for nearly four hours, first one taking the advantage and then the other. Robin's left arm bled where the friar had wounded him and round one of the friar's assembly of chins was a dripping necklace of blood.

Both men were blinded by their own sweat. The weight of their chain-mail, unnoticed before, now hung on their bones like lead. The muscles of their sword arms burnt in agony. Twice Robin had thought he saw the friar's head swim into space and it seemed that he had sliced the friar's neck clean through, but each time when he blinked his eyes the friar's head was firmly attached to his shoulders again and his sword still aimed at Robin's head.

Then, as Robin came forward in a renewed attack, the friar stumbled. In falling he caught at Robin's shoulder and both men sank to their knees. For a second neither spoke, then, wiping the sweat out of his eyes, Robin cried to the friar to give him permission to blow his horn.

"Gladly," agreed the friar, "if you give me leave to whistle when I will."

"Granted," said Robin, and sent the note of his horn singing over the river.

In minutes the six outlaws came into sight, running full speed to their master's aid.

"My men," said Robin gleefully.

The friar took one glance at the running figures, set his fingers to his lips and blew through them in a loud whistle.

"My dogs," he said, as from the direction of the Abbey came a pack of cur dogs. There were some ten or twelve animals, all powerful as mastiffs. Some had smooth coats, some shaggy, but all with jaws like mantraps and eyes intent on their master's enemies on the other side of the river.

The outlaws, seeing the dogs, fitted arrows to their bowstrings and let fly, but the dogs leapt into the air, snatching at the arrows and crushing them in their jaws as they ran on at the outlaws.

Little John, seeing two of the great dogs leaping up at Robin, jaws slavering, came charging across the river, his broadsword held aloft, crying death on the curs. Yet when he reached his master's side a roar of laughter burst out of him and he grasped the friar by the waist and swung him off his feet.

"Whistle off your brutes," Little John cried. "Would you attack your friends? Even the gross and turgid Tuck would not stoop so low."

"John Little," cried the friar, and setting his fingers to his lips he whistled until all his dogs had returned to him and were frothing round his heels like so many sheep.

"You have met my good master, Robin Hood?" said Little John.

"Indeed," said Friar Tuck, looking ruefully around at the trampled reeds and muddied ground. "If I had but known who he was I could have spared myself this necklace." His fat fingers touched the wound at his neck.

"And had I but known who you were," said Robin, grasping Friar Tuck by the shoulder and hand, "I had not given it to you. I set out this morning with only one thought in my head – to find the great swordsman Friar Tuck and bring him home to Sherwood."

The friar's bead-black eyes twinkled with merriment and he smacked his fat lips together in amazement.

"This morning," he said, "I had fully intended to take myself and my hounds to Sherwood. Winter comes on apace, a lonely time for a solitary man. When I had downed that last pie, had I not been called upon to carry a certain

65

C

rogue across the river, I would have been on my way to Sherwood to search you out."

"Come with us now," said Robin. "Be my man."

"That I will. To share your fire, an ale mug and a good tale will set the winter by its heels. I'll come."

So they set off back to Sherwood. Robin, Friar Tuck and Will Stukley walking together, the hounds ranging before and behind them, while the other outlaws listened to little John's tales of Friar Tuck's reputation as a story-teller, and his venison pasties and game pies.

Soon they were swallowed up by the early evening shadows, lying like pools of dark velvet under the golden trees. The water meadows were silent when they had passed. A chill breeze rippled the reeds. Autumn stood on tip-toe, waiting to be gone, while winter moved down silently from the high northern lands with snow falling from his robes and icicles in his hoary beard. Hard days were coming when life would be cruel for men living in caves or under bare forest trees. Food would be scarce and men would learn the trick of tightening their belts.

But that night, as the outlaw band lay sprawled around their fire, ale warming their hearts, and the booming voice of Friar Tuck acting out for them the fall of the walls of Jericho, not one of them gave a thought to the coming cold.

CHAPTER SEVEN

Tam Barley was the outlaw in charge of the band's money, and in late October he came to Robin with a coffer that was half empty and a sorry tale to tell.

"There was new cloth for our winter clothes," listed Tam as Robin, Little John and Will Stukley listened to his account. "Grain for flour. The village of East Rive sore pressed by that villainous baron the Duke Legronde – each household to receive a silver coin by your command."

Robin nodded his approval. Even with a silver coin to make up for the money that had been taken from them in taxes, most families would hardly survive the winter without starvation and death knocking at their doors.

Tam continued his list: leather and pots, salt and spices, physic and arrowheads.

"None wasted, master," declared Tam. "I keep as close a watch upon this money as if it were my own."

"Perhaps it is time we had a few more guests to dine with us," suggested Little John, and Will Stukley grinned his agreement, both knowing that any who were invited to dine with Robin Hood never refused the invitation or a drawn bow would know the reason. All who dined under the great oak were asked to pay for the privilege. Many a poor peasant paid no more than a feather or a pebble he had in his pocket, but the rich travelled on their way, having left their money bags in Tam's good keeping.

"True," agreed Robin gravely, for he had not realised that their funds were at such a low ebb. Then his face brightened, and turning to his companions he said, "Shall we invite the Sheriff of Nottingham to dine with us?"

"Aye," said Little John. "Go and knock him up and bid him attend our feast and bring his gold with him."

"He will surely come," agreed Will Stukley, "running to set his gold at our feet."

Robin Hood sprang up. "The Sheriff will come," he promised, "and this very day. Prepare a feast for him and he will come riding at my side, bringing his gold with him as a gift."

On hearing Robin's words the three men threw back their heads and roared with laughter. Other outlaws, hearing their laughter, came over to find out what it was about and soon some fifty of the band had gathered around, telling each other that Robin was to bring the Sheriff of Nottingham to dine with them that very afternoon.

"One thing," said Robin as he picked up his bow. "Wat, Will Poor and Ham Docken, see to it that the deer herd freely about our camp. I should not like to bring the Sheriff here and have him think that our larder is empty."

The young men Robin had named looked at each other in surprise.

"We shall bring the deer from the whole of Sherwood," they promised. "But tell us why."

"By this afternoon you shall know," said Robin, and turned to leave his men.

"Master," called Little John, springing up to be at Robin's side. "I see you are taken by some hare-brained scheme, but do not go alone. Take me and some others with you."

"By no means," said Robin. "I go to Nottingham to invite the Sheriff to dine, and the sight of such a mountain as yourself moving at my side would drive his few wits from him and he might forget to bring his gold. But I shall take Tod with me if he promises not to scare the Sheriff." Then Robin went off to dress himself in the finest clothes he could find in the hut where the outlaws kept their disguises.

Although it was still very early morning, the road leading to Nottingham was astir with folk, for today, as Robin knew, was market day in that city. Robin and Tod sat down to wait by the roadside in the shelter of a clump of bushes, sitting so silently that none who passed noticed them. Even a blackbird who landed on a twig close to Robin's head sat there singing and then flew off without spying them.

It was almost an hour before Robin saw the pony and cart for which he was waiting come trotting towards him at a brisk pace.

"Blithe morning, Jem Ross," cried Robin, stepping out from his cover.

"Why, master," exclaimed the man who was driving the cart. "What brings you here?" He drew rein at Robin's side.

"Your pony is lame," said Robin. "Bring her in from the road until we check her foot for bruises."

"Aye, she has been lame since we left home," said Jem Ross, winking, and allowed Robin to lead his pony and cart into the shelter of the trees where they were hidden from the road.

Jem Ross was a butcher and his cart full of meat bound for Nottingham market. Last winter the Sheriff had taken Jem's younger brother prisoner and had it not been for the outlaws' money he would have been a prisoner still.

"How can I help?" Jem asked.

"I have a mind to play butcher for a day," said Robin. "Will you lend me your pony and cart?"

"Gladly," said Jem, jumping down and handing his reins to Robin while the black pony cropped the grass, wondering to herself what had taken her master's mind that morning when normally he laid about her with voice and reins if she suggested stopping for a mere mouthful.

"Wait here," Robin told the butcher. "Before night Tod

will bring your cart back to you and tomorrow one of my men will bring you payment for your meat."

Jem nodded, wondering to himself what plan Robin had in his head, but he only said, "Good luck to you," as Robin drove off.

Robin Hood and Tod reached the market and found themselves a place amongst all the other butchers. At first the other butchers looked suspiciously at Robin and his fine clothes, knowing he was a stranger whom they had not seen before.

Robin stood by his cart, shouting his wares in a loud, clear voice, and as the other butchers listened, their suspicions changed to hostility, for Robin was selling his meat at less than a quarter of the market price. Soon Robin's cart was crowded round with housewives.

"For such an fair cheek and smiling lip I'd give my meat away," Robin said, piling the meat on the scales and making all the women press closer about his cart.

Two of the other butchers elbowed their way through the crowd.

"What lunatic are you to come to market to give your meat away?" one of them demanded.

"Charge a fair price," the other snarled, "or the dogs will have your meat when we have kicked over your cart."

"Fie," cried Robin in mock alarm. "Let the dogs have the wretched stuff." He picked up a leg of lamb between finger and thumb and threw it to a cur dog who was sniffing amongst the carts. "'Tis none of my choosing that I am here. Did I ask my uncle to die and leave me his filthy meat?" He snatched a handkerchief from his sleeve and held it delicately to his nostrils.

"Pray do not vex yourselves. After today you shall not see me here again," he continued, and went on giving away his meat for next to nothing.

The Sheriff, riding through the market place, noticed

the crowds about Robin's cart and sent two of his men to investigate.

"Some prodigal with more money than sense," reported the Sheriff's man. "He has fallen heir to his uncle's butchery, considers it beneath him and is giving the meat away to be rid of it."

The Sheriff's eyes narrowed. "Bring him here," he ordered.

"Why, right gladly," said Robin when he was told that the Sheriff wanted to speak with him, and telling Tod to look after the pony and cart he minced his way to the Sheriff.

When he reached the Sheriff Robin swept him a low bow, lavishly twirling his feathered hat through the air in wide circles.

"Take a care," the Sheriff cried as his horse reared away from Robin. "Give me your name and your business. Come explain yourself."

"You see before you," cried Robin, pulling the wide brim of his hat well down over his face, "a hapless man. What has my uncle chosen to do but die and saddle me with his wretched meat and pastures full of horned beasts all on the hoof. I ask you what shall I do? I cannot give the stuff away – and as for those herds!"

The Sheriff looked at Robin, seeing only a fool in front of him.

"Gladly would I give those beasts away if I could find someone generous enough to take them."

"How many head?" asked the Sheriff greedily.

"Why, half the number of horns," cried Robin. "Lack, sir, I have more to do than count the creatures." Again Robin sighed gustily. "Though my uncle's will states that there are more than three hundred."

"Would you sell?" asked the Sheriff, bending down over his horse's shoulder.

"For four hundred pounds I would sell the land they
71

graze on as well," Robin assured him. "I promise you, sir, I am in desperation to be rid of them."

"Let us discuss it further," said the Sheriff, looking hastily over his shoulder in case anyone should have overheard this fool offering to sell land and cattle at a fraction of its value.

Over the Sheriff's best Malmsley wine they discussed the deal.

"One thing," said Robin, "I must be rid of the beasts tonight, for tomorrow I set out back to London. If you would buy them you must ride with me now to see them, bringing your money with you. If this is too sudden I must find another kind soul to taken them from me, for I swear I shall not stay another day in this sodden backwater," and Robin made to rise.

"Stay, stay," cried the Sheriff. "The deal is settled between us. I shall ride with you this hour."

"And the price?"

"In my men's saddle bags."

So it was that while Tod drove the pony and cart back to their owner, Robin, mounted on the Sheriff's second-best horse, followed by two of the Sheriff's men, their saddle bags clinking with gold, led the Sheriff straight into Sherwood.

"Had you warned me that your uncle's lands lay in this direction I would have brought more men with me," said the Sheriff, looking about as they rode closer to Sherwood. "Being a stranger to these parts you will not have heard of Robin Hood and his gang of cut-throats who make our lives a torment."

"I have heard of him," said Robin.

"It surprises me little. The misdeeds of such a villain are bound to be common gossip, even in London. This, then, is the very forest where his band has their hiding place."

The Sheriff urged his men to keep a good look-out for

any signs of the outlaw. "You are sure this is the way to your uncle's cattle?" he demanded nervously when Robin turned his horse to follow a track winding between the trees.

"Quite certain," laughed Robin. "In a little while you will see more horned beasts than you had dreamed possible."

The Sheriff felt a sudden icy shiver creep over his scalp and up his spine. In a second everything about his companion seemed to have changed. He had lost his foppish, uncertain air. Before, he had sat his horse as if more than half afraid of it. Now he sat boldly in the saddle, his hands firm on the reins, looking about him in a commanding fashion.

"Almost," thought the Sheriff, "as if he were a lord coming back to his estates." At this thought the Sheriff's blood froze in his veins and his teeth chattered with fear. For it *was* a kingdom into which he was being led. It was Robin Hood's kingdom of Sherwood.

Robin, realising that the Sheriff had at last seen through his disguise, laughed aloud in the Sheriff's face.

"Look," he cried. "Here they come – the horned beasts you are here to see."

Through an opening in the trees passed a great herding of deer.

"Arrant rogue and scoundrel," raged the Sheriff. "Your lies and cheating set this trap."

"No, no. Only your own greed brought you here," said Robin, as the forest was suddenly alive with men.

"As I promised, I have brought the Sheriff to dine with us," he cried. "Come, lead us to the feast."

Only Robin and his men feasted, the Sheriff and his men sat tight and frozen with fear, expecting every moment to feel an arrow in their backs or hear a knife drawn from its sheath to slit their throats.

"Though I fear our feast has not been to your liking,

73

still, my good Sheriff, it is the rule of this place that you must pay. Men, how much has our guest to offer us?"

The two outlaws who had been counting out the gold from the saddle bags brought it before Robin.

"Four hundred pounds," they told him.

"It will pay for the food they have eaten," said Robin. "But would have been poor payment for the beasts and land they thought to buy with it." He signalled to his men to take the money away.

The Sheriff and his men remounted their horses, were blindfolded, as they had been when they were brought to the oak, and were led away.

"Visit us again," called Robin. "You are always welcome as long as you pay for your supper."

The outlaws' mocking laughter rang in the Sheriff's ears as he was led hither and thither before his blindfold was removed, and with a great shout and waving of arms the outlaws who had been leading their horses startled the animals into a runaway gallop through the forest. All the road back to Nottingham the Sheriff said not one word, but the resolve hardened in his black heart to kill Robin Hood by any means, fair or foul.

"How neat one of my arrows would have looked, sticking out of his evil throat," said Little John later that night when he and Robin were sitting together, staring into the wood ash embers. "Only last week I heard how he gave orders for a peasant to be hung in front of his wife and children because he was a week late in paying his taxes. Not because he had not paid them but because he was one week late in bringing them to the Sheriff."

"And I," said Robin, "saw a peasant shot through both legs, hamstrung. Had my men not found him he would have died of starvation in the forest. The Sheriff's men had discovered him with a longbow in his hand, a hare slung from his belt."

"Pagh," cried Little John in disgust. "And you would not let me shoot him!"

"Would you have my deeds as dark as those of the man I despise?" asked Robin. "Just before I came to Sherwood I killed a Forester and I vowed to Our Lady that I would never kill another man unless in the most dire necessity of self-defence."

"They are not men but lice," said Little John.

"No, they are men," said Robin, getting up slowly and making his way to the shelter where his bed of bracken and deerskins waited for him.

And although he went over all the cheering things that had happened that day – the tricking of the Sheriff, the full coffer which meant a secure winter for the outlaws and the neighbouring peasants, and the way the blackbird had perched so close to him while they had sat hidden that morning, scattering his song into the world for all to hear – Robin could not shake off the melancholy that had settled round him like a wet cloak while he had been speaking to Little John.

Try as he might, Robin could not touch the source of it. He could not find out what caused it – whether it was the knowledge that another summer had gone by and still he had not dared to try to find Marian again, whether it was the fact that Richard Lion Heart, who was now king of England, had gone to the Holy Lands to lead the crusades, leaving his own kingdom to be torn into bleeding shreds by his false brother, the regent John, his Norman Barons and the greed of the churchmen, Robin could not say. As he turned away from thinking, it seemed as if his sadness was a dim, shadowy thing, waiting for him in the future, a shadow from which there could be no escape.

CHAPTER EIGHT

Winter passed, turning as it always has into spring. The outlaws had fared well, being short of neither ale nor venison, nor wood to heap upon the roaring flames as they sat around the fire, listening to Friar Tuck's endless tales. Many poor folk had blessed the name of Robin Hood when they found a coin, slipped beneath their door by night, to buy food for an ailing child or to pay an apothecary to ease an old man's pain. But once February was over the outlaws began to shake off their winter ways and long for the first days of April.

It was on the first of these spring days that Robin and Little John were returning from an expedition to a fish pond in a neighbouring hamlet, with over a dozen speckled trout lying cool and luscious in the shade of a wicker basket. They strode back to their camp, marching step for step, singing as they went, their eyes filled with the green of new leaves, the flicker of birds' wings and the half-seen shimmer of blue where the bluebells would soon carpet the forest floor.

"Listen," whispered Robin, laying his hand on Little John's arm and drawing him into the cover of the bushes. "Someone comes and I do not think it is one of us."

Both men fitted arrows to their bows and waited. They heard the stranger before they saw him, and from his singing voice knew him to be a youth. Clear and sweet, his song rose to the April skies as he sang the praises of his love. Little John, glancing at Robin, saw his face grow gentle with longing and knew that he was thinking of Marian.

The youth came into sight and he was all that a young

lover should be – tall and slender with a clear-cut face, deep blue eyes and nut-brown hair that fell in soft waves to his shoulders. He was clad from head to toe in scarlet, a brave, proud colour, bright against the spring green. On one shoulder he carried a harp and on the other a bow and arrows.

While Robin and Little John watched, he lay down his weapons and his harp, then threw his cap with its scarlet feather high into the air, where it whirled and flashed like an exotic bird. The youth let it lie where it fell while he leapt and bounded about the clearing, turning and spinning, feet in the air, head over heels.

Then he stood quite still. "Ellen," he said, "Ellen," as if the name were the most wonderful thing in the whole world.

At length he set his cap back on his head and, picking up his things, went on his way, the joyful notes of his song still reaching the outlaws' ears long after he was out of sight.

"They call it love," said Little John, "though I know naught of such high passions. Yet I know the lad who has caught such a pox of it."

"Who is he then?" asked Robin, only half listening, half dreaming of Marian's dark eyes and long auburn hair.

"Allan a Dale, they call him. A travelling minstrel. He came this way last autumn and fell in love with Ellen, daughter of a wealthy yeoman. I think he returns to marry her, though I doubt if her family will approve of the match."

"Lucky fellow," said Robin, "if the lass is half what he believes her to be at this moment." He walked on in silence, no longer noticing the spring forest all around him.

The outlaws enjoyed the fish so much that next day Robin and Little John went back for more. As they were returning, they approached the same glade where yesterday they had seen the young Allan a Dale. Today a strange sound met their ears. Fitting arrows to their bows, they crept stealthily forward.

Lying flat on the ground, his face buried into the grass, lay Allan a Dale. His bow, arrows and harp were flung carelessly from him and the sound they had heard was the sound of his weeping. The feather in his scarlet hat was broken, and from what they could see of his bold, gay clothes they looked as if he had been wandering through the forest in them all night.

"Why, what a change!" exclaimed Robin softly.

"I doubt he has found the lady false-hearted," murmured Little John, a grin twitching the corners of his mouth.

Robin stepped into the clearing. Aiming his arrow at the prostrate figure, he told him to stand up and cease his noise.

The lad leapt to his feet, attempting to snatch up his bow and arrows.

"Too late for that," said Robin. "Only a fool casts aside his weapons in Sherwood. Have you not heard of the wicked outlaw, Robin Hood?"

"Aye, and thought him a right true man," said the youth.

"Give us your name," said Little John, joining his master.

"They call me Allan a Dale."

"So I thought," said Little John. "We saw you yesterday go leaping through the forest like marsh fire."

"Ah, yesterday . . ." said Allan as if it were five hundred years ago.

"And today you weep like a babe. What ails you? Has she proved false, for by your song of yesterday we know there is a lass in your heart."

"Ellen, false?" cried Allan. "That she is not. She loves me as truly as ever. If she had changed her mind, why then she must have gone her own way. But it is her father who has changed her mind for her. She must marry a rich old man – Sir Gilbert of Mey. He has not a tooth in his head or a hair on his skull. He is all a-shake and a-dangle and a-drool. And he shall not have her. I say he shall not have her." The youth smashed his clenched fist into the palm of his other hand as he spoke.

"What says Ellen?" asked Robin.

"They have shut her away so that we cannot see each other. Only a glimpse of her have I had, when I climbed the roof and peered in all the windows, until I found where she was imprisoned. No sooner had I found her than they found me. Knocked me from the roof like a ripe chestnut and set the dogs upon me."

Sadly the lad surveyed his spoiled clothes.

"But she shall not marry him. I swear it. Yet I do not know how I am to stop them forcing her to the church and to this marriage."

"How did you think to stop it by lying in the forest, weeping?" asked Robin.

"I was not weeping," Allan said, denying all the evidence. "I was 'sore set to with grief' as the ballads say." He paused, and looking straight at Robin went on. "I care not whether you think this Robin Hood a rogue or not. I am here to find him for I think there is no one else could rescue Ellen for me. Then I remembered how they all say that Robin Hood demands gold for his services and I was sore set to with grief, as you discovered me."

"They speak falsely who say this of Robin Hood," declared Robin angrily. "He takes only from the rich. What riches do you have, Allan a Dale?"

"Riches?" laughed Allan scornfully. "Why, I have no riches. I spent all I had on these clothes for my wedding and this ring which was to have been Ellen's wedding ring."

Allan a Dale took a gold ring from his pocket which he laid on the palm of his hand and regarded sorrowfully.

Then, squaring his shoulders and pushing back his hair, he put the ring securely back in his pocket and said, "I am sure you are right. Riches will not matter to Robin Hood. Let me pass and I shall seek him out and swear to be his true man as long as I shall live, if he can find a way of saving Ellen from her father and that ancient weazen. A faithful heart and a strong arm will mean more to Robin Hood than all the gold in a king's ransom."

"Well said." Robin grasped Allan a Dale by the shoulder. "You need search no longer. Robin Hood stands in front of you."

Allan a Dale dropped on to one knee, doffing his hat with the crumpled feather.

"Stand up," said Robin. "We will need all the brains we have to rescue this Ellen of yours. No time for grovelling. Now tell us, is she a lass of spirit?"

"Indeed she is."

"Then we shall find some way of saving her. Come, let us go back to our camp and lay our plans."

Early next morning, three groups of people made their way to the little church where Ellen was to be wed to the aged Sir Gilbert.

The first to reach the church was Sir Gilbert of Mey and some dozen of his friends, relatives and servants. They helped Sir Gilbert from his litter and guided the old man's steps into the church where the Bishop, fussing and bothering and thinking of the rich gift which Sir Gilbert would undoubtedly give him when the ceremony was over, settled the old man into a pew at the front of the church.

"Is she not come yet?" demanded Sir Gilbert testily, looking back up the aisle with rheumy eyes. "If she be a tardy wench we must cure her of it. Aye, cure her sharply."

From the next group to reach the church only one man went inside, the others crouched, hidden, behind tombstones. The one who went in was a tall man with a light step and a merry twinkle in his hazel eyes. He carried a harp in his hands and strode boldly into the church as if he had been an invited guest.

"What would you here?" demanded the Bishop. "Are you a friend of bride or groom that you march in so sure of a welcome?"

"I come to bring music to this wedding," said the stranger. "To brighten up what would be a sorry affair without me."

"Stay then," said the Bishop. "And play your harp now for here is the bride." He hurried back to the altar to help Sir Gilbert to his feet.

At the church door, Ellen's father dismounted from his horse and lifted Ellen down from the saddle where she had been brought to church, held firmly in front of him. No friends or relatives had come with them for they all considered that he did Ellen a desperate wrong to force so old a man upon his daughter.

"Give over your tears," warned her father sternly. "I have found you a good match. Many a lass would be grateful to have such a rich husband."

But Ellen's heart was as heavy as lead and tears flowed from her blue eyes like fountains as she thought of Allan a Dale, her only true love, whom she would never see again.

"Come, dry your eyes and cast the thought of that vagabond out of your mind."

"Father, I beg you . . ." pleaded Ellen for a last time, but her father gripped her tightly by the elbow and forced her into the church.

For a moment the darkness of the church after the brightness outside blinded Ellen as she searched desperately for the old man who was to be her doom, but before she could pick him out a stranger was standing in front of her. Surely a stranger, for she could not recognise him, and yet the harp he carried belonged to Allan a Dale. Some tiny part of Ellen had kept hoping until this very last minute that somehow Allan would find a way to rescue her, but when she saw his harp in another's possession the last, faint, hopeless hope died.

"Harper, if you are here to play, give us your music," ordered the Bishop.

"That I will, but first I must ask the bride for her choice. What tune would she have at her wedding? An old tune or a new?"

The harper bent close to Ellen as if listening to her choice.

"Be of a bold heart," he mouthed. "Your true love waits outside to be your groom. How say you? Speak your love."

Fair Ellen's heart rose like a bird set free.

"Yes, oh, yes," she answered.

"Out of our way, rogue," cried Ellen's father while Sir Gilbert demanded to know why the shrewish wench was not yet at his side.

"Play if you are here to play or take your wretched frame out of this church," said the Bishop, losing patience.

"Yes, I am here to play. A merry tune to put right the wrongs of this marriage that you are about to commit."

With this, the harpist flung back his cloak, revealing his clothes of Lincoln green, at the same time taking his horn from his belt and blowing a long clear note on it.

Through the church door came a dozen of Robin's men, arrows fitted to their bowstrings. At their head came Allan a Dale and with one sure movement of love Ellen was in his arms.

"You see here the two lovers whose wedding day this shall be. Young maid was never meant for old man. We come to right the wrong. Friar Tuck, up with you to the pulpit and conduct this marriage," cried Robin.

The longbows and true aim of the outlaws held back Sir Gilbert and his friends, Ellen's father, frothing at the mouth with rage, and the pop-eyed Bishop.

"Stop! You rogues and vagabonds!" squawked the Bishop as Friar Tuck climbed solemnly into the pulpit. "This shall not be."

"He is as holy a son of Mother Church as yourself," Robin assured him.

"But the banns have not been called," declared the Bishop. "Three times they must be cried."

"Why then, I shall cry them seven times," promised Friar Tuck and did so.

"I do," said Ellen, her voice tender as a ripe pear full of sweet juices, when Friar Tuck asked if she would take Allan a Dale.

"I do," said Allan a Dale, and gathering up his bride kissed her full on the lips.

So they were wed and went back with Robin Hood and his band to live in Sherwood, leaving behind them a church buzzing like a hive of angry bees.

The wedding feast went on all through the night, and dawn was breaking when Robin left the feasting and walked a little way into the forest to sit alone, thinking of Marian.

CHAPTER NINE

"What ails you, master?" demanded Little John with ill-concealed irritation, for he and Robin Hood were out to shoot deer for the outlaws' store pantry and for the second time that morning Robin had missed a buck that had been an easy target.

"My bow loses its truth," said Robin flatly.

But Little John was too annoyed to listen to such an excuse.

"There is naught wrong with your bow," he insisted stoutly. "More like it is you who lose your own truth."

Robin glowered fiercely up at him. "Take care how you speak to your leader," he said sharply.

"Then let our leader take care how he speaks to us," replied Little John. "It is three weeks now since we saw Allan a Dale married to his Ellen and since then you have been as dull as a November mid-day. We have had company enough. Two Norman barons who gave us a song and a gay dance." Despite his annoyance, Little John grinned, remembering the stately foreign grace of the two terrified French lords. "We led those Foresters a merry chase, leaving them in Daunton's marsh to find their own way out of it. And is that not a bold tale which Friar Tuck is telling us of King Arthur and his knights?"

But Little John's words brought no answering enthusiasm to Robin's face.

"There," exclaimed Little John in disgust, "you are as dull as November." And lifting his staff he rattled his master about his head.

Instantly Robin gripped his own staff, swinging it wildly, and going at Little John with such a temper that the giant was hard pressed to defend himself.

"Take that, and that, and that," cried Robin, battering Little John about the shoulders. "A pox on your November days and your interference. Forget not who is master in Sherwood."

Robin swung his staff with such force that Little John's mighty cudgel splintered like tinderwood and the shock of the blow shattered through the giant's huge frame. But Little John only roared with laughter. "A December gale has cleared away your November mists," he said. "Why, this is more like your old self."

Robin shrugged his shoulders. "My temper only covers up the truth you speak," he admitted, "for I am not myself these days."

Little John, seeing that their fight had loosened his master's tongue, sat down on a fallen log. Taking the ale skin from his waist, he held it out to Robin.

"To make a shrewd guess at your complaint, I would say your trouble is your heart," he said when they had both drunk from his ale.

Robin nodded ruefully.

"And to give it a name, why, I would choose the name Marian."

"Aye," agreed Robin. "You would be right. I have only glimpsed her once since I came to the greenwood. Yet she is as close to my heart as ever she was." He stared dolefully into space.

"Then go and find her and bring her to Sherwood," said Little John. "Now Ellen is here she would make a fine friend for your Marian."

Robin shook his head. "What have I to offer her? How could I ask her to marry me now? In the old days I was Robin of Loxley and now am a common outlaw."

"Common outlaw you are not. Were King Richard to return from the crusades, all would change. His lily-livered younger brother plots only to steal the kingdom while Richard is fighting the Holy War. We do no wrong when we take from the corrupt Church and grasping barons to give to the common people. Methinks Marian would join you gladly for such a cause. Give her the chance to choose for herself. From what you have told me of her, she loves you truly."

As if Little John's words had filled him with new resolution, Robin stood up, grasped his staff in his hand, slung his bow and arrows on his back and turned to face Little John.

"You speak well," he said. "If Marian be the maid I knew she will come to Sherwood. I have been mad to doubt her."

"Do not go undisguised," warned Little John.

"I will go as I am," said Robin. "With my hood pulled over my face no one will know me."

Although Little John would have liked to warn Robin further of the risks he ran in returning to where he was well-known without wearing a disguise, he saw that his master's mind was made up and so said no more, only wished Robin good luck as he disappeared from sight between the trees.

"He would not wish to go courting, wearing the rags of a beggar," Little John thought, smiling to himself.

Marian was the daughter of a wealthy merchant, Thomas Mortimer. When Robin had lived at Loxley Hall, Marian had lived some ten miles distant in a large stone house known as the Willow Winds, named for the river that ran through its grounds. Many times Marian and Robin had wandered together on the river bank, under the dappled sun and shade of the willows, and shared lazy summer days, watching for the flash of a kingfisher's wing or the flickering silver of trout seen in the shallows. There had been winters when the river had frozen over and they had held feasts on the ice, the torches spurgling smoke and flame into the darkness while their skates whispered on the frozen surface, and May mornings with Marian riding at his side and the little hawks hanging motionless above the meadows.

As Robin strode through the forest, memories of these carefree days came back to him and he realised how he must have changed during the years he had spent in Sherwood. A reluctance, a kind of shyness, came over him.

"She will see me as a wild man of the woods," he thought, and changing his direction he decided to go first to Loxley Hall, which he had not seen since the Abbot had driven him from his home.

Robin walked slowly up the long drive to Loxley Hall. Each step brought back memories of his childhood.

"Whoever it is that the Abbot has installed in my rightful place takes scant care of the grounds," Robin thought. "Or of the house," he added, as a turn in the drive brought Loxley Hall into full view. Overgrown bushes, rank grass and weeds surrounded the Hall whose roofs and doors cried out for the care of a loving craftsman.

Robin pulled his hood further down over his face, intending to knock on the door of Loxley Hall and ask for bread and a draught of water, but before he could reach the door a thick-set, low-browed man came running from one of the outbuildings, waving a stick at Robin and shouting at him to be off.

"A drink from your well, good master," said Robin. "I fear to drink from the river in case it carries the sickness. And a crust of bread for my belly."

"We give no alms here. Get you gone or the dogs will see to it that your throat needs no more water."

"If you refuse me water," said Robin, "at least tell me the name of your master."

"And what is that to you?" the man said, coming closer to Robin, trying to see the face hidden in the shadow of the hood. "What is it you want here? You look to me a right saucy knave."

The man's hand shot out, pulling the hood from Robin's head.

Before he fully realised what he was doing, Robin had fitted an arrow to his bow and aimed it at the man's heart.

"Take care before you lift your hand to a stranger," Robin cried. "Do not make a habit of tweaking off hoods when you do not know what you will find beneath them."

The man, now a quivering slob of fear, had fallen on his knees before Robin.

"Prithee, I meant no harm. Put aside your bow. I am but my master's servant. It is on his orders that I let no one near the house. I must refuse all requests for alms. Drive all away."

"Who is this generous master of yours?" asked Robin, thinking of past times when no one was ever turned away from the doors of Loxley.

The servant sat up on his heels to answer, his pale eyes intent on Robin's face as he spoke.

"The land belongs to the Abbot of St. Maries, but my master, who only stays here when he is not travelling about on his business, is Guy of Gisborne."

At this name a cold sweat burst out of Robin, a loathing of disgust and shame blackened his mind, his hands shook and his bow almost dropped to the ground. He turned swiftly away from the man kneeling in front of him and pulled his hood back over his head as he strode away from Loxley Hall. His first feelings of shock changed to a blinding rage that such a creature as Guy of Gisborne should be living at his former home.

Guy of Gisborne was known throughout the land as a most foul murderer. His skill with the longbow and broadsword almost equalled Robin's own and there was nothing that he would not do for gold. He would kill woman or child in cold blood, track down a victim to France or the Netherlands until one of his black arrows winged his back. It was well known that both noblemen and clergy employed Guy of Gisborne to carry out their baser desires.

So enraged was Robin that he did not hear the muted

sounds that followed him down the drive. He did not look back to see the servant watching, half hidden in the gateway, to make sure that Robin was going in the direction of Loxley before he took to his heels over the fields to Loxley village, making straight for the inn where a number of the King's Foresters were usually to be found.

At the doorway of the first cottage that Robin came to, an old woman sat, silver hair wisped over a pink scalp, twisted hands folded in acceptance on the rough cloth of her skirt. At her feet lay a black hound, her heavy head couched on her outstretched legs, her muzzle sprinkled with white hairs. Robin was so embittered that he walked like a blind man, seeing nothing, and he would have passed them had the hound not lifted her head and scented him. Then, with a howl of unbelievable delight, she came leaping at him, prancing and pawing the air, tongue licking, tail threshing and eyes shining with joy. Nearly knocked from his feet, Robin was jolted back into the present moment.

"It is," he cried. "It is Meg. Meg!" The hound, hearing her name spoken by her master, went into a fresh fit of delight.

The old woman watched without moving, her eyes as blue as speedwells and as clear as a child's.

"The dog knew better than me," she said. "I would have let you pass without knowing you, Robin of the Wood, or as I think men call you now – Robin Hood."

Robin looked closely at her. "Nurse," he said, the childhood word difficult in his mouth.

He took her hand, kissed her on the frail cheek and, sitting beside her, listened while she told him all that had happened at Loxley. How all the servants had left, drifting away although the Abbot would have had them stay. How the Hall had lain empty but was now used by Guy of Gisborne when he was in the district.

"Although he seldom stays more than a week or two, being about the country on his butcheries," said the old woman. "But enough of him. What brings you back after all this time?"

Robin told her how he had come to find Marian again and had resolved to ask her to be his bride and live with him in Sherwood if she would have him.

"Aye, she would have taken you, I'll be sworn to that. Many a time she came to talk to me of the old days and somehow it was always yourself we talked about. Never another man would she look at." The old nurse nodded her head, smiling. "No one else for her. But you come too late." She reached down to feel the comfort of the black hound lying at her feet. "Her father, his business prospering, grew weary of country life and has taken the family to London. They went in the autumn before Goose Fair."

"How shall I find her in London?"

"You may save your boot leather, for we have heard that she is to marry a rich young scholar who will make a fine match for her."

Only a few minutes before, Robin would not have believed that the day could carry more misfortunes for him, but at his nurse's words his spirits sank like a stone, and when he walked on into Loxley he felt himself to be the most cursed of men.

His old nurse and the hound dog, Meg, stayed where they were, watching him go. Both would have had him stay, yet neither moved to follow him.

Robin trudged through the village, all his thoughts turned inward on his own misfortunes, seeing nothing of the villagers who turned to stare at the hooded stranger. Only once did he look up out of himself to see a young lad coming along the road towards him. He was riding a bay pony that trotted along at the dusty side of the road. The lad had suntanned skin and brown pansy eyes. His hands on the reins were as light as a maid's. When he rode past there was a brightness about him that pierced even Robin's gloom.

"The world cannot be all black," Robin thought as he stood for a second, watching the pony trot out of sight with its young rider sitting straight and easy on its back.

"All goes well for some but not for me," he thought as he walked through the village and on down the road.

Robin had barely lost sight of the last of the cottages when his sixth sense told him that something was wrong. He looked around sharply and saw behind the clump of wayside bushes that he had just passed the glint of steel caught by the sun. Just in front of him grew two ancient beech trees, one on either side of the track. A quick glance upwards showed Robin about six Foresters, partly hidden in the lower branches of the trees.

There was the imitation of a bird's call, almost drowned by the sound of Robin's horn calling to any outlaws within earshot to come to his aid.

"There he is. It is him. Robin Hood!" cried the triumphant voice of the servant from Loxley Hall, and almost before Robin had time to draw his sword he was surrounded on all sides by Foresters.

There was no past and no future, only the present moment where Robin's sword struck and drove like a living thing. This was no mock challenge but a fight for life. To be aware of the men crowding him from behind as well as in front. To feel the receiving flesh as his sword bit into the Foresters' bodies.

Two men dropped wounded at Robin's feet and for minutes they served as a barrier holding back the more timorous souls. Robin danced light on his toes, knowing that his only chance of survival lay in his ability to keep moving. He felt blood running past his right eye and knew from the pain that he had also been wounded in the arm. Yet hardly knew, hardly felt it. There was only the searing, hectic dance of the surviving moment. Moments that somehow joined together into a chain, link by link, to give the outlaws time to come to Robin's aid.

A swarthy, pock-faced man came up close to Robin, his lips drawn back from yellow teeth, his sword flashing. At the same time Robin was struck by a blow from behind and felt pain spread beneath his shoulder blades. He knew that if his men did not come soon he could not hold out any longer. He saw the cell in Nottingham jail, the sneering satisfaction in the Sheriff's eyes.

Again the swarthy Forester struck with a shrewd blow. Robin took it on his sword but fell to his knee with the shock of it. At once three Foresters were on top of him, but Robin battled to his feet again, shaking himself free as if the men were terriers clinging to a bull.

Yet Robin knew that his strength was failing and he listened desperately for any sound that might signal the approach of his men. He heard the hooves of a pony being galloped flat out along the road. For a second Robin glanced away from the fight and saw the lad who had passed earlier bearing down on the Foresters with a drawn sword in his hand. He was leaning from the saddle to swing his sword at heads and faces as he passed, only to turn his pony round in a rearing halt and ride to the attack again and again.

"Right welcome you are, though I know not your name," cried Robin and went at the Foresters with renewed fury.

From the trees, ten outlaws came racing to Robin's aid and the Foresters took to their heels, carrying their wounded with them. A rain of arrows from the outlaws' bows followed them down the road.

"They took me in an ambush," admitted Robin, looking shamefacedly at his men, "and would have had me prisoner but for your coming, and the aid of this young man."

The lad had dismounted and was leaning over his pony's neck. As Robin turned to thank him and ask his name, the youth slumped to the ground in a dead faint.

"He is wounded," cried Robin and ran to the lad. He crouched down, cradling him in his arms. The hat the

boy had been wearing fell from his head and auburn curls cascaded down his back.

"Marian," cried Robin and could not say another word for the tightness in his throat.

Marian's eyes opened.

"Are you hurt?" cried Robin.

"Not one scratch," she assured him. "If I fainted it was for joy, not wounds. Joy that I have found you again."

"But how is it that you are here?" Robin asked, Marian lying sweet in the crook of his arm.

"I had come to find you. Nurse told me that you had gone this way and when she said it, I knew that I had passed you. I came full speed."

"And saved my life."

"I could not stay in London. I have taught myself to use bow or sword as well as any man. I've come to prove to you that I am fit to live in Sherwood."

"And I set out today to find you and bring you to Sherwood as my bride."

Friar Tuck married them in a brave ceremony beneath the great oak, and the outlaws, all in Lincoln green, raised a mighty roar to cheer Robin Hood and his maid Marian.

Through that summer the happiness of Robin and Marian seemed like a full-bloomed flower as day followed day of sunshine, freedom and good fellowship. Often as Robin lay on the sward, staring up through a dazzle of leaves with Marian by his side, he would think all things perfect, and batten down the knowledge that Guy of Gisborne still had the use of Loxley Hall.

"It does not matter now, now that I have Marian," Robin told himself, but he lied.

CHAPTER TEN

Little John and Robin Hood walked side by side along a forest way. Rain slanted from a heavy sky and the ground was mire beneath their tread. It was early morning but no birds sang and no small animals scuttled through the undergrowth. The two men seemed the only beings alive under the arching boughs of the forest.

"Dreams," said Little John, "are caused by rotten meat and bearded cheese. They come to us all and we forget them. The real things are here." He struck his fist against the trunk of a beech tree and stamped his foot into the muddy ground.

"This was such a dream that it could not be forgotten. I was alone on a windy plain and although I turned from it the wind grew stronger, driving me where it would have me go. I shut my eyes against it, but when I was forced to open them, a black horse barred my way and I knew that I must kill it."

"A tosh to your dreams, I say," declared Little John, who was heartily sick of the whole subject.

"It seemed," insisted Robin, "that there was something more evil than the horse, but that when I had killed it this other would be dead too."

"If you will not leave your dreams, then I shall leave you," said Little John. "There is a widow woman in Erlton village who seeks our aid. She had been cruelly wronged by the Sheriff and begs us to help her." Little John paused, expecting Robin to insist on coming with him.

"I am certain it was a black horse," continued Robin, "yet the wind blew so strongly and with such an evil will that I cannot be sure."

Little John hit him a good-humoured blow between the shoulders. "I leave you to your dreams," he said. "I go to Erlton and we shall see, come night, who has had the better day." So saying, Little John went his way and left Robin Hood alone.

Robin walked on slowly. He turned from the path and made his way through the bushes and dense undergrowth. Almost any other man would have found it impossible to pass where Robin went, but his years in Sherwood had taught him how to move through the forest as if he were a fox or a shadow.

Treading silently, his mind still vexed by the strange dream that haunted him into the day, Robin came to a small copse of hazel bushes. In autumn it was a favourite place for the boys of the camp to come nutting. Looking round the bushes, Robin saw that the nuts had already grown round and brown and he knew it for one more sign that summer was drawing to a close. He plucked three of the nuts, cracking them between his teeth and they were sweet to his taste. For a moment he cradled the split shells in the palm of his hand and then tossed them to the ground.

Where they fell, the body of a young boy lay in the long grass. A black arrow, flighted with black feathers, stuck out from his back. The lad was wearing Lincoln green, soaked to a darker shade by the rain and stained with blood.

Robin knelt swiftly beside him, but he was cold and stiff with death.

"Diccon, the Sheriff's page," said Robin, letting the boy's face sink back into the grass. "God rest you."

Blowing his horn, Robin summoned his men.

"Shot in the back," cried Will Stukley. "A swine to shoot thus and at an unarmed lad."

"Take him and bid Friar Tuck give him a Christian burial," said Robin. "I shall go on until I find the man who loosed such a coward's arrow."

97

"They say that Guy of Gisborne shoots such black arrows. That they are the mark of his trade," said one of the outlaws. "I have seen them before."

"I, too, have heard this," said Robin.

"Do not go alone," pleaded Will Stukley. "Take at least four men with you."

The outlaws, horrified by the death of the page and the dark name of Guy of Gisborne, crowded round Robin, anxious to go with him.

"I go alone," said Robin, turning away from them. "Let no man follow me for this unsett steven* is my bane."

When Robin left his men he followed the trail of the man who had shot the page, without any difficulty. No attempt had been made to hide the tracks and to Robin's eye it was as clear as a road to market.

Robin came to a glade surrounded by birches and hazels. All his instincts told him that he was close to his quarry. He stopped, still hidden by the trees, and looked out into the clearing, and the sight he saw there froze his very heart's blood.

"Now Our Lady and all Saints protect me," whispered Robin, crossing himself, for in the glade was the figure from his dreams.

In front of him stood the shape of a man clad from head to foot in the hide of a horse. Mane, tail and ears remained in place. The skin from the head formed a cowl that hid the wearer's face. The hide gleamed in the downpour but Robin could see that the skin had been cured and tanned and was now like plate armour, protecting the wearer. The man moved and Robin saw that his quiver was full of black arrows. Without hesitating, Robin strode into the clearing.

"Good day," he said. "Although I know not whether I speak to a man or beast."

The man swung round to face Robin, one hand closing on the hilt of his sword. He pushed back the cowl from his

* Unsett steven=odd chance, unlooked-for opportunity.

head and revealed a face as evil and dark-visaged as any that Robin had seen in all his days. Black eyebrows sprouted in a single bar above his pale jackdaw eyes, his nose curved like a hawk's beak while his mouth was a tight, lipless line.

"Take a care how you speak," the man snarled, "or your tongue will be a little red fish in the grass. Give me your name." His voice growled with hunger, the hunger of the ocean greedy to swallow the land.

"My name is of no matter," said Robin. "I live in the forest, minding the King's deer."

"You are such a man as I seek."

"That may be so," replied Robin.

"Being of the forest, you will know of this Robin Hood?"

"Aye."

"And what of him? Tell me or your guts will garland my sword."

"They say he shoots a straighter arrow than any in England and few can hold their own against him with the sword."

Jeering, mirthless, laughter poured from the horse skin. "You speak to one who can. I am Guy of Gisborne and I care not who knows it. Shudder and grow pale. You will not be the first to shrink from my name."

"If I shudder," said Robin, "it is not from fear but from disgust that so fair a place as Sherwood should be darkened by the sound of that name."

"It is a name to make weaklings tremble. The Sheriff holds it in such high esteem that he has promised me any boon I crave when I have killed this Robin Hood. He will know the deed has been done when he hears one blast on my horn where he waits, close by Erlston, holding a merry hanging. And he shall hear it this day. Already I have taken a treacherous pageboy who deserted his master to play at outlaws."

At the thought of the boy shot in the back, Robin grew cold with a terrible rage.

"What a bold man it must take to kill a boy," he said slowly.

"There is not anyone living whom I would not slay for gold. Nor any place throughout the length and breadth of England that has not felt the death blow of my sword or the blood-letting of my arrows," and he leered through the falling rain at Robin.

"Yet this glade has not seen the flight of your arrows. If you think to take on Robin Hood, you had best practise first with one of his countrymen."

"That I should draw my bow against the likes of you," scoffed Guy of Gisborne.

"Lest I tell willing ears how you feared to accept my wager?"

"Set up your mark," said Guy of Gisborne, "and look to yourself when I claim my winnings."

Robin cut and peeled a hazel branch. He stuck it in the ground, then, stepping back, he challenged Guy of Gisborne to hit it, using two arrows only.

"Now I know you for the mad being you are. None could hit a wand from such a distance."

"It is my challenge," stated Robin.

Guy of Gisborne shot first, and both his arrows missed the mark by some twelve inches.

"It is an idiot's mark," he growled scornfully. "Take your turn and then you shall feel my sword about your crazy head."

Robin took his place, he fitted the arrow to his bow-string and took careful aim. His first arrow missed the hazel wand by a finger's breadth.

Calmly he drew back his second arrow, knowing that this time he would split the wand, knowing that when he had done so he must draw his sword and fight Guy of Gisborne to the death. Since he had killed the Forester on

the day he had been driven from Loxley Hall, Robin had kept his vow and killed no man, but he knew now, as his dream had told him, that he must fight Guy of Gisborne and rid the land of this evil being.

The arrow flew sure from Robin's bow to split the hazel wand. Even as it struck the target, Guy of Gisborne had drawn his sword. Staring through the empty eye sockets of his horse's head cowl, he fell upon Robin.

Robin had been expecting some such treachery and leapt round to face him, his sword whistling through the air.

"Black-hearted villain," cried Robin, taking the crash of Guy of Gisborne's sword on his own blade. "Know that you have met your match. Dance now to the metal of the sword of Robin Hood."

Through the grey, impersonal rain, the two men fought, giving and taking blow for blow. Each knew that the other was set to kill, and that whichever way the fight went, death would be present at the end.

Guy of Gisborne slipped on the wet grass and stumbled forward. Robin drew back to let him find his footing again and Guy of Gisborne, pretending to be struggling to his feet, made a desperate lunge at Robin's legs.

"Foul creature," cried Robin. "You are indeed as black as men call you."

As Robin fought, his dream stayed in his mind, how there had been no way for him to go except to kill the horse. "It was meant as an omen, telling me clearly that I must break my vow and kill this man."

Then Robin put from himself all clinging reluctance to take another human's life. Collecting all his strength, he went at his enemy, and striking with a sure blow, pierced the horse skin hide and drove his sword deep into the black heart. With a terrible groan, Guy of Gisborne sank down, his cowl fell back and he lay dead.

Robin drew out his sword and wiped it clean on the wet grass.

"It was time that your evil deeds should trouble the earth no longer," he said. "Mine was the hand chosen for the work."

Although Robin knew that no man could blame him for killing such an evil being, he felt a great sadness come over him and he knew that now his vow to our Lady was broken, everything must change.

"We must not keep the Sheriff in suspense," Robin said. Stripping the horse hide from the dead body, he put it on over his clothes of Lincoln green. Then, taking Guy of Gisborne's sword, bow and arrows, he dragged the body from the clearing and laid it out of sight where it would never be found again.

"Now," thought Robin, "I shall take the horn and bow of Robin Hood as proof that he is dead and see what advantage may come of it."

CHAPTER ELEVEN

When Little John left Robin, he went at full speed towards the village of Erlton, where the widow woman lived who had sent a neighbour to Sherwood, beseeching the outlaws to come to her aid.

Stopping at the first cottage in Erlton, Little John asked if they knew of a widow who was being cruelly treated by the Sheriff.

"And that I do," answered the woman who had come to the door. She pointed to a small cottage set some way back from the village street. "You'll find her there – the Widow Dawson – or like you'll hear her first. Poor soul has not stopped weeping since they took her sons away. That people should stand by and see such wrongs done!"

Little John went to the cottage that she had shown him and as he turned towards it he heard the sound of sobbing. When no one answered his knock, he pushed the door open and went inside. An old, white-haired woman was sitting with her elbows on a scrubbed, wooden table, her head buried in her hands as she wept bitterly.

"Good day, mother," said Little John by way of greeting.

"Let no man call this day good," said the old woman, "for today they will hang all three of my grown sons. Fair lads and tall, each one of them, and there is not a thing I can do to stop them. I have sent word to Sherwood, begging the good Robin to come to my aid, for they say he has tricked the Sheriff many times, but if he comes not soon he will have to raise the dead, for at the noon hour they hang my sons," and she buried her face in her hands again.

"I have come from Robin Hood. Tell me your story as

104

quickly as may be. Then I shall find some way to outwit the Sheriff and free your sons."

"I am right glad to see you and beseech you to bring my sons back alive, for they are good lads . . ."

"Mother," said Little John, "tell me your tale. How did your sons fall into the Sheriff's hands?"

"Not last night but the night before, his men came shouting and knocking at my door. We four sat at our evening meal. When we did not answer on the minute they came bursting into the house. One broke into the pantry and found salted venison there. They demanded to be told who had shot the beast, but when my eldest boy admitted to the crime – if crime it be, for the beast was taken in the winter when food was hens' teeth and I lay sick, so I say it was no crime but an act of Christian charity such as Our Lady would bless whole heartedly . . ."

"And then?"

"Why, then they said they did not believe him and took away all three of my sons. Yesterday they brought me news that all are to be hung from a forest tree and their poor bodies left dangling there to teach others a lesson." The old woman gave a low groan of despair.

Little John laid his great hand on her shoulder.

"I shall find some way of freeing them," he promised her. "Do not weep any longer, instead, find me a cloak and a leather jerkin with which I may cover up my Lincoln green!"

The old woman went away quickly and returned with the clothes which had once belonged to her husband. Although they were all too small for Little John, they served to disguise his outlaw's clothing, especially a long cloak which covered him from shoulder to ankle, and a felt hat with a wide, soft brim.

"When I return I shall have your sons with me," Little John promised.

One of the villagers directed Little John to the place in

the forest where the boys were to be hung, and he went there as fast as he could, knowing that it must be close on mid-day. He stopped only once, by a still pool, to smear his face with dirt and bedraggle his hair. Then he cut a short stick for himself so that he might walk with it and disguise his height.

When he reached the place in the forest where the hanging was to take place, Little John saw that he was indeed just in time. The three youths were kneeling on the ground, their hands bound behind their backs, ropes around their necks, the ends of which were flung over a bough of the tree above them.

"Now, by my troth," muttered Little John, "would that Robin had not dreamt that dream, then he would be here with me." For Little John could see no way of saving the three young men.

Some three dozen of the Sheriff's men were in the clearing, and the Sheriff of Nottingham himself was there, sitting astride a grey horse. Just as Little John was thinking that the only way he could save the boys would be to hide in the undergrowth and, as they were being slung aloft, to shoot them down, crying out to them to run for their lives, one of the Sheriff's men came up behind him and asked him his business.

"I am an old man," said Little John in a cracked voice. "A holy Palmer. One who takes no part in the ways of the world."

"Strange then that you should be here when a hanging is about to take place. Have I not seen you before?"

Little John bent closer over his stick. "I go about the villages, selling my herbals and holy charms."

The soldier's suspicions were not satisfied.

"Let the Sheriff take a look at you," he said, and took Little John across to where the Sheriff, with a scowl on his face, was waiting. Having strung up his prisoners, he now had no one to hang them and he was unwilling to ask one of his own men to undertake such degrading work. His eye brightened when he saw the cloaked figure being brought towards him.

"Who have we here?" the Sheriff asked.

"An old man calling himself a Palmer," replied the soldier, and Little John clutched closer to his stick, wishing he shared his master's tricks of disguise.

"Old man," said the Sheriff, "would you earn yourself an honest sixpence?"

"That I would."

"Then be you hangman to these three rogues and I will give you one."

"No," said Little John. "Never have I stooped so low. I would not touch such work." Then a sudden thought struck him that made him change his mind.

"Have they been shriven?" he asked piously. "Has a man of the Church heard their last confessions?"

"We have no time for that," said the Sheriff. "They must speak to St. Peter for themselves."

"It is not right for any man to meet his death unshriven. If you will let me hear their confessions then I shall play the part of hangman."

"Make haste, then," said the Sheriff unwillingly, and Little John made his way to the three youths, gathering his cloak about himself for fear that any should see his clothes of Lincoln green.

"Draw back," Little John said to the Sheriff's men. "It is not fitting that any save a holy man should hear the last confessions of another. Give a thought to the hour of your own death," he added as the men stepped back. "I see it crouching close to each one of you."

"Make no sound," Little John whispered, leaning over the first lad. "I am from Robin Hood and have come to save you." Under the cover of his cloak he cut the thongs that bound the lad's hands. "Let no one see that I have cut your ropes. Stay as you are until I raise my bow, then toss the noose from your neck and make all speed into the forest."

All three youths were too relieved to move a muscle, for all had given up life and prepared themselves to die. So cunningly did Little John move that neither the Sheriff nor his men suspected anything.

When Little John had made the sign of the cross over the last man, he sprang back in a powerful leap, fitted an arrow to his bow and aimed it straight at the Sheriff.

"They are free men," shouted Little John standing up to his full height as the three youths made for the safety of the forest. "They have the freedom of Sherwood." And his cloak fell open, revealing his clothing of Lincoln green.

"Arrest the outlaw," cried the Sheriff, and six of his bravest men made a dash at Little John.

Little John took aim at the foremost of them, meaning to loose his arrow then escape into the forest while the men tended their wounded comrade. He drew back his bow-string, there was a rending crack and the trusty bow that had served him so faithfully lay at his feet in two parts.

In minutes the Sheriff's men had overpowered him, although it took ten of them to hold him. They bound him securely and dragged him before the Sheriff.

Just as the Sheriff was about to speak, they heard the sound of a bugle horn. Little John knew that it was not Robin's horn, but the Sheriff's face lit up at the sound.

"Here we have the servant," he crowed, "and unless I am mistaken that horn tells me that the master is taken as well."

"None could take my master," cried Little John. "And be not so sure that you have the servant."

"I have both," sneered the Sheriff. "You will make a pretty pair, hanging side by side in Nottingham."

Through the trees and into the clearing came a man in horse's skin armour which was cut about and stained with blood. On his back he carried the bow and black arrows of

Guy of Gisborne, and in his hand the bow, arrows and horn of Robin Hood.

"Where is your prisoner?" demanded the Sheriff. "Did I not hear your bugle note which was to tell me of your victory."

"You did hear my horn and it tells you of my victory. I have killed that evil man," replied the grating grind of Guy of Gisborne's voice.

"Then, Guy of Gisborne, you have done right bravely," said the Sheriff, his face like a thundercloud with the sun shining behind it.

"You lie," cried Little John. "One such as you could never kill Robin Hood."

"Is this not his bow? These his arrows? And this his horn?"

Little John looked at his master's things and could not deny them.

"And do you think that Robin Hood would part with them unless he was dead?"

Again Little John could give no answer, for he knew most certainly that Robin would never have given his arms into the hands of such a man as Guy of Gisborne.

"You speak truly," sneered the Sheriff, and a deep satisfaction glowed in his heart to think that at last his hated enemy was dead and would trouble him no more. "Claim your reward. I promised you anything within my power to grant."

The man inside the horse skin did not hesitate for a second. Looking straight at Little John, he said, "The prisoner you have, is it not the man they call Little John, the close companion of Robin Hood?"

"Indeed it is," said the Sheriff with satisfaction. "To-morrow in Nottingham he will know the taste of the gallows."

"Not so. I ask as my payment to be given the enjoyment of carving up his bulk of a man. He is too good to hang.

Tomorrow would be too late. It would not be the first time that a prisoner has escaped from the jail at Nottingham. Tie him to the tree and I will show you what sport can be had from a skilful killing."

The Sheriff's men turned away in disgust. They would have been glad to see Little John hang, but they were revolted by the cruelty of Guy of Gisborne. Even the Sheriff was reluctant to grant such a grizzly request.

"Take gold," he said. "Take land. You have earned them."

"I have your word," said the grim voice. "Anything within your power to grant."

"Tie him to the tree," ordered the Sheriff and turned his horse away.

When Little John was securely bound, the figure in the horse skin drew his sword. He leant over Little John, testing the knots.

"Take courage," he mouthed, and with a surge of unbelieving joy Little John knew that the horse hide contained not Guy of Gisborne but Robin himself.

"As I lunge at you I shall cut you free," Robin told him. "Groan horribly and they will not have the stomachs to watch."

"He is well secured," Robin said in a loud voice and stabbed at Little John with his sword.

Sickened by the grotesque shape of the man in his horse-hide covering and the groans of his victim, the Sheriff's men drew away and many were filled with loathing for the cruelty of Guy of Gisborne. Even the Sheriff found something of particular interest to watch in the opposite direction.

With a final accurate stroke, Robin set Little John free, gave him the bow and arrows that had belonged to Guy of Gisborne, and in that instant both men were racing for the trees, taking it in turns to cover each other's escape.

When they were safely under the cover of the forest,

Robin turned and shouted, "Next time you see a horse hide, be not so sure that the beast is within."

When he realised how he had been tricked, the Sheriff let out a terrible oath. Setting spurs to his horse, he galloped at full speed back to Nottingham. He raged into the castle, screaming for wine, then knocked the goblet from the page's hands as he grabbed the flask and set it to his lips. With a roar of fury that reverberated throughout the castle, he threw himself this way and that about the room, overturning chairs and tables, tearing tapestries from the walls and matting from the floors. He foamed at the mouth like a mad dog, clawed his nails down his arms and tore at his hair, so maddened was he that once again Robin Hood had outwitted him.

Once they were safely back in the depths of Sherwood, Robin stopped by a deep pond covered with emerald green scum. Stripping off the foul horse skin, he threw it into the pond and watched it sink slowly beneath the green slime.

"Our tales of today's adventures will hold still even the tongue of that fat friar," said Little John.

"They will," said Robin, turning to walk on. "It has been a day that was waiting for us."

Through the trees came three of the outlaws, and with them Sir Richard of Lea, an old knight whom Robin had helped in the past.

"What news?" called Little John, knowing from the knight's appearance that he came with a purpose.

"Great news," replied Sir Richard, his eagle face thrust forward, his white beard and hair shining like a halo about his face and head. "I have heard that King Richard is to return to his own land, to England."

"Would that you have heard truly," said Robin, filled with hope that Sir Richard's news might be true, that the King might return to his people.

It was the final touch in this day of change, this day that had been waiting for him.

CHAPTER TWELVE

All through the winter and spring rumours of King Richard's return ran like wildfire throughout England, but the summer brought news that the King had been captured and was being held prisoner in Austria. It was not for another two years, after the English people had paid a great ransom for his release, that King Richard was able to return to his own country. A juggler who had come north for the May Day fair brought the news to Nottingham, swearing that the King had landed on English soil.

The July sun, striking through the oak leaves, made shimmers of light on the ground about the great oak. Venison, fish and game boiled and roasted over the outlaws' fires. Newly-baked bread sat on wooden trays and barrels of ale waited to be opened. The outlaws had heard that a party of black-robed friars and their Abbot were making their way along the west road. The Abbot was mounted on a stalwart chestnut horse, the friars on mules, and from each friar's saddle hung money bags that clinked sweetly as their mules trotted along.

"To let them pass through Sherwood without an invitation to dine, that would be churlish indeed," said Robin when his men brought him the news. "Prepare a feast worthy of our visitors while I go to meet them."

Robin took some twenty of his men with him and strode out through the forest to greet his guests.

"Would that I had a draught of good English ale to quench this thirst," said the Abbot. "My throat is parched dry by this heat. I would give half the gold in our money bags for a drink."

Robin Hood and his men stepped out in front of the riders and Robin laid his hand on the horse's bridle.

"Who are you that bar our way?" demanded the Abbot in a voice without any trace of fear.

"I am Robin Hood. These are my men. We dwell in the greenwood, guarding the King's deer and righting wrongs as he would do were he here."

"Indeed," said the Abbot. "We are pleased to hear it."

"Passing by, I heard your longing for a drink of ale. Come and bring your men with you and you shall not want for a jug of ale or a game pie before we set you on your way again."

"An invitation so forceably thrust upon us could not be refused," said the Abbot. "But we will come with you gladly."

Robin's men surrounded the little group of friars and with Robin walking by the Abbot's side they went straight to the great oak.

"Why, what a kingdom," cried the Abbot as he looked around. "King Richard himself would not be ashamed to feast with you here."

"Nor any more welcome," said Robin, and the outlaws who had heard the Abbot's words chorused their agreement.

When their guests were seated on fallen tree trunks Robin asked them if they would not push back their hoods and reveal their faces.

"That we may not do," said the Abbot. "We are all under an oath to Our Lady that we shall not remove our hoods until our mission is completed."

Several of the outlaws had moved forward to take off their hoods by force but when Robin heard the Abbot's words he signalled that they should be left alone.

"A vow to Our Lady," he said, "was ever held sacred here."

He called for meat and ale to be served to their guests.

Unlike many of Robin's guests, the Abbot and his friars ate heartily and drank well.

"Now," said Robin, "the time has come to pay. All who dine here must pay for the cost of their meal so that their gold may be shared amongst the poorer people and so the world goes round. If I am not mistaken, you offered half your gold for a draught of ale."

"I did," said the Abbot, "and since I have received far more than ale I must pay more. Take what you will from our money bags."

"For that brave speech I give you back the gold I would have taken. Few indeed have offered Robin Hood more than that for which he asked."

But Tam Barley, who was sitting close to Robin, looked on the tall, regal figure of the Abbot with suspicion. He knew the value of gold and he did not trust any man who gave away his money with such an open hand.

Tam watched the Abbot closely. His hands, half hidden beneath the flowing sleeves of his robes, were rich with rings. They did not look to Tam like the rings of a churchman, even a wealthy Abbot would not flaunt rings like those that glittered on this man's fingers.

A thought came into Tam Barley's head – a thought so incredible that Tam, who was not given to fancies, was quite astonished at himself. But once the thought had arrived it refused to leave. Tam looked shrewdly at the five friars and saw that one of them whose habit was somewhat askew, was wearing striped hose of scarlet and yellow.

Tam Barley got quietly to his feet and slipped away from the feast. He hurried through the forest to find the hunting party of Sir Richard of Lea. Tam had seen it earlier in the day and he knew that Sir Richard was the only person who could help him with this ridiculous notion.

"A song," cried Robin when the plates were empty and ale jugs full again. First Marian sang a song of love, then Tod a crude song of a bold hunter who went out to take a boar and was gored in every possible part of his body, and then Allan a Dale took his harp and sang one of the true tales of his master, how Robin had played butcher and tricked the Sheriff.

At first, as they listened, the Abbot and his friars showed no signs of amusement, but when Allan a Dale sang: "How like you my horn'd beasts, good master Sheriff? They be fat and fair for to see," the Abbot and his friars laughed as loudly as the outlaws.

"Now," cried Little John, when Allan a Dale had finished his song, "let us set up a target and shoot for the sport of it."

The outlaws reached for their bows, while Robin twisted a garland of elm twigs and hung it from the trunk of a beech tree.

"Let all stand the distance of the third mark," he said, "and show our guests how straight a bow we men of Sherwood can draw. Any whose arrows fall outside the garland shall receive a buffet from Little John."

At this the outlaws turned to each other, raising eyebrows and shoulders, for the third mark was a great distance from the target and many feared they would feel Little John's fist about their ears before they were much older.

Little John shot first and his three arrows all found their home safely within the circle of elm. Thirty outlaws took their turn and of the thirty only three felt the iron hammer of Little John's fist.

"The King of England would be proud of such a bodyguard," said the Abbot, watching the shooting intently.

"And proudly would we serve him," said Robin.

"Light words easily spoken," said the Abbot. "Would you leave your Sherwood for the King?"

"For King Richard, the true King, we would go gladly. There is not one man here who would not crave a pardon from King Richard were he here."

For the next round, the outlaws stood still further back

115

from the garland and many, including Will Stukley and Allan a Dale, felt the iron buffet of Little John's fist.

When all had shot they cried to Robin Hood that he should shoot too.

"By your leave," Robin said, leaving the Abbot to take his stand further from the target than any other outlaw.

The sun was hot and the ale strong. Robin's first and second arrows flew true but his third hit the tree, outside the garland. A groan of dismay mixed with laughter ran through the outlaws as they saw the arrow miss its target.

"How now, little master," grinned Little John. "You must take your buffet. Prepare yourself for the blow."

"Not so," said the Abbot, rising to his feet. "It is not seemly for a man to hit his master. I shall deliver the buffet."

"Had I but known there was a choice, I think I should have chosen the Abbot," mumbled Allan a Dale, his head still ringing from Little John's treatment.

The Abbot drew back the sleeve of his robe, displaying the glitter of gold and jewels on his fingers and the iron-hard muscles of his arm.

"Come," he said to Robin. "You deserve this for the gold you have stolen from me." He hit out with such a blow that Robin was knocked to the ground.

As the Abbot struck Robin, his black cowl fell back from his head and he stood uncovered, as Tam Barley and Sir Richard of Lea, with two of his noblemen, hurried into the clearing. Instantly Sir Richard of Lea fell to his knees, and drawing off his hat cried, "Your Majesty!"

As the two other noblemen knelt down, Robin slowly swam back to his senses. He opened his eyes to see a tall, broad-shouldered man standing in front of him. The sunlight glistered on his hair and beard, his blue eyes were hard as sapphires and his mouth was curved and strong-willed. He took off his Abbot's disguise, and his doublet, encrusted with gold embroidery, outshone the sun itself.

"It is the King, our true Leige and Majesty," cried Sir Richard of Lea. "I have not seen your Majesty since I fought at your side."

"The King," echoed Robin kneeling before him. "Richard Lion Heart, true King of England."

As if a wind blew over a field of grasses so the outlaws knelt before the King. Robin set his horn to his lips, summoning all his men until the whole space in front of the oak was filled with kneeling men. Only the King stood upright.

"Mercy, your Majesty," said Robin. "As you know we are all outlaws here and our deeds are black in the eyes of the Sheriff and the Church, but never have we been anything but loyal to the true throne of England. Grant us your pardon and we will serve you faithfully and well."

King Richard placed his hand on Robin Hood's shoulder.

"Stand up," he said. "True bowmen of England, I will grant a free pardon to each and every one of you, if you, Robin Hood, will bring with you five score of your best archers and serve me faithfully as my own bodyguard."

"Right gladly will I do that," said Robin as the outlaws cheered, and in the glamour of the moment he saw it as a brave and noble thing to do, to leave Sherwood and visit foreign lands in the service of this golden King.

"Then, to all you men of Sherwood, I grant you my royal pardon."

Sudden excitements and laughter blistered through the outlaws, the ale flowed and the sun blazed down and so they feasted through the afternoon.

"I think that the life you lead in Sherwood would have been much to my liking," said the King as he wiped tears of laughter from his eyes.

"It sounds in the telling a merry prank," said one of the King's nobles sourly.

"Should we have one last jest upon this Sheriff of Nottingham?" the King said, leaning towards Robin Hood.

Little John and Friar Tuck heard the King's words and pricked their ears.

"So that he will not forget you," laughed the King. "Do you have spare suits of Lincoln Green?"

"That we do," replied Robin, his blood rising at the thought of any trick to be played on the Sheriff.

From the forest of Sherwood, along the road to Nottingham, flowed a sea of men all dressed in Lincoln green, all with longbows in their hands. At their head rode Robin Hood and King Richard. The people of Nottingham, seeing this flood of outlaws bearing down upon them, cried in panic that Robin Hood and his band had left the forest and were coming to lay seige to their city. Some locked and bolted their doors, some grasped their children by their hands and fled, while others lined the road to cheer.

Right up to the walls of Nottingham Castle came the outlaws and found the gates fast barred and bolted.

"Knock upon the gates," commanded King Richard, "and tell the Sheriff we have come to visit him."

Little John took his cudgel and beat a rain of blows upon the gates.

"My master bids you open and let us in," he cried. "Or we will break down your gates."

The Sheriff, seeing all the outlaws taking openly to the streets, was sure that the King, who had dined with him the night before, had been killed. He came to a window, a trembling, whey-faced figure, and looked down on the nightmare below him.

"Open your gates," cried the King, pulling off his hood of Lincoln green. "I and my bodyguard will dine with you tonight."

So the Sheriff of Nottingham entertained all those who had once been outlaws in Sherwood. He sat sourly watch-

ing them devour his food and wine, neither eating nor drinking himself.

And although it was a jest much to Robin's liking, he too drank little, and ate less, for tomorrow the King was to return to London, taking Robin and his archers with him.

CHAPTER THIRTEEN

For one long year and three long months, Robin Hood served King Richard, and each day his heart grew heavier until his longing for Sherwood was like a millstone that he dragged with him everywhere he went. The life of the court sickened him with its falseness and double dealing. Food lost its taste, wine its spirit, the scented air of the court was too flaccid for breath and even his love for Marian and his skill with the longbow brought him no joy. Always, no matter what else he was doing, he thought of the greenwood, and often when he was alone the words spoke themselves aloud – "Sherwood. Sherwood."

Within the first six months, nearly all the outlaws who had come to London with Robin had returned to Nottinghamshire. Some crept away without a word, others made awkward excuses. Even Little John and Allan a Dale had left. The King had been sorely displeased to see his bodyguard slipping away in this fashion and had forbidden Robin to let any more of his men leave. Although Robin had listened to the King's command he had not had the heart to stop any of his men doing what he so longed to do himself.

One morning in October, Robin was walking in the grounds of the King's Palace at Westminster. His mind was on Sherwood, thinking how the forest would be fired with autumn, chestnuts and hazels falling ripe from the trees and the cobwebs on brambles and bracken diamonded with dew. He thought of the taste of mulled ale, the crackle of winter fires and Friar Tuck's voice telling his tales.

The sound of young men's voices broke through his

thoughts and Robin saw that five or six courtiers had set up a target and were shooting at it. For a moment Robin watched their clumsy archery and careless timing which lacked all precision; so slovenly that he would not have accepted it from the youngest lad in Sherwood.

Suddenly Robin went over to them, and taking one of the young men's bows and a full quiver, he stood back three times the distance from which they had been shooting. He set an arrow to the bow and it flew as if of its own accord, straight to the centre of the target. Robin shot two more arrows and they lay close to the first, forming a tight triangle. He paused, and was aware of the watching silence of the young men, the brightness of the morning and the reality of Sherwood waiting for him to return. He took a fourth arrow, and drew back the bowstring to let it find its place in the middle of the other three.

Without a word Robin gave the bow and arrows back to the youth and, turning went straight to the courtroom. He sat there with the other petitioners waiting for King Richard. When the King arrived Robin took his turn, and knelt down before the King.

"May it please your Majesty to grant me leave to return to Sherwood," Robin said. His mind frothed with imaginary reasons but he waited without making use of any of them.

The King scowled, drawing down his brows. He was little pleased with the outlaw band. Away from their own forest they had proved to have little discipline, and as they practised less so their skills with the bow declined.

"So you too would run away?" Richard asked. "Next month we set sail for France. What will you do then, my bold Robin Hood?"

At the King's words Robin bowed his head. He knew that whatever happened he could not go to France without seeing Sherwood again.

"Sire, give me leave to go."

122

"For seven days," said the King. "Then you must return to me."

Without delay, Robin saddled horses for himself and Marian and set out for Nottingham. When they reached Nottingham they spent a night with Sir Richard of Lea and Robin left Marian there in the knight's safe keeping while he rode on alone to Sherwood.

He left his horse with a peasant in the village where he had first met Little John and walked on to the plank bridge where they had fought together for the first time.

Robin stood on the bridge and gazed at Sherwood. All about him the trees welcomed him home. Bronze and golden with autumn, the leaves spread a fire carpet for him to tread and the dark shadows whispered of contentment and rest, of peace and good company, of days gone by.

He went into the forest, touching the living trunks of the trees, letting the fern fronds curl through his fingers, standing with breath indrawn to see the passing of deer, smelling the damp fungus as his feet followed the old ways that would bring him to the heart of Sherwood where the great oak reigned supreme. Before he reached the oak, Robin took off the clothes he had worn at court and dressed himself in the Lincoln green which he had kept with him since he left Sherwood.

At the oak, Robin set his horn to his lips and blew three blasts.

"How many times my men have answered that call," he thought and his heart ached for the high, bold days of the past.

Little John reached Robin first.

"Why, what do you do here?" cried Robin, flinging his arms round his companion.

"Where else would I be?" cried Little John. "We knew you would come back."

In twos and threes the outlaws came running to greet their master – Friar Tuck and Allan a Dale, Will Stukley and Tod – until the forest was ringing with the name of Robin Hood.

They built huge fires and held a great feast with archery and ale and told tales of the time they had spent apart. The seven days' leave which the King had given to Robin flew past on wings, but Robin paid no heed to their passing, for long before the seven days were over he had forgotten all about his promise to return. Richard and his court had vanished from Robin's mind, less substantial than the dawn mists.

Through time the King sent his soldiers to join with the soldiers of the Sheriff of Nottingham and drive all the outlaws from the forest, but even King Richard's might could not win against green shadows who aimed deadly arrows and vanished through the trees.

For twenty years Robin and his band lived the free life of the greenwood. New men, joining them, others returning to the life they had left. Marian died of a fever and when she was gone Robin grieved sorely, for the world without Marian seemed a hollow, empty place. His bow lay idle and for the first time younger members of the band were able to outshoot their master, and, although they had not noticed it before, they became aware of Robin's age.

"My flesh is heavy on my spirit," Robin said to Little John as they sat together. "A sickness gnaws at my bones. It comes to me that my cousin, the Prioress of Kirklees Abbey, is skilled at the letting of blood and mine these days is of so bad a hue I would have some taken from me."

"To go into an Abbey is to put your head in a noose. All churchmen hate us and most would see us dead. We have played too many jests on them for any to treat us well."

"She is my kin," insisted Robin, "and would do me no harm."

In the end he persuaded Little John to go with him to Kirklees. It was a long journey to the Abbey, and by the time its towers came into sight Little John was all but carrying his master and was sick at heart to feel his weakness.

The Prioress came to the Abbey door and was little pleased to see her outlawed cousin. She listened to Robin and agreed to blood him in the hope that it would cure his sickness.

"Do not go with her," whispered Little John urgently. "Do not trust her." He could see the evil, scheming mind of the Prioress disguised beneath her nun's robes and her folded, white hands. "Come back to Sherwood."

But Robin, leaning heavily on the Prioress's arm, went with her into the dark of the Abbey. When Little John tried to follow them the Prioress told him to remain outside, and Little John, who could have tackled ten men single-handed, stood and watched his master taken up a stone stairway, then he turned away to wait in the Abbey grounds.

The Prioress laid Robin on a bed in a stone cell at the top of the stairs. Skilfully she cut an artery in his arm so that he might bleed, then she went out of the room, locking the door behind her.

Robin lay and felt his strength flow out of him but gradually, as the Prioress did not return, Robin realised that she had left him to die. He struggled to sit upright and staunch the flow of blood, but he was already too weak and fell back in a swoon.

When he came to himself again, Robin rolled from the bed to the floor. Stretching out, he just managed to reach his horn and draw it towards himself. Clasping it in his hand, he dragged himself across to a slit window and, pushing himself up on one elbow, he put his horn to his lips. He blew it for a last time – a sad weak note that made Robin laugh it was so feeble a thing.

But Little John heard the sound. He sprang up and tore through the Abbey grounds, raged into the Abbey, scattering the flutter of nuns, and raced up the stairs where he had last seen Robin. At the top of the stairs he came to a locked door. Setting his shoulder against it he charged through it into the room.

A bloody sight met his eyes, and in the midst of the shambles his beloved master lay by the window, his horn fallen from his hand.

"Master," cried Little John, "what deed has brought you to this? Come, I shall carry you back to Sherwood."

"Too late," said Robin, his voice a harsh breath of sound. "I beg you fit an arrow to my bow. I would draw it for one last time."

Little John did so and supported his master in his arms while Robin took aim through the window and sent his last arrow soaring into space.

"It flies!" cried Little John, watching the arrow, but Robin sank back into his arms, exhausted.

"Bury me where it falls," he whispered and felt the heavy drag of his own death tightening on his heart. He would dance the greenwood dance no more and fear opened like a pit at his feet.

Then a moment from his childhood came back into Robin's mind. He was a boy standing at the roots of a great oak, the springtime bright about him. A fallow buck and two does came into the clearing as he watched, stepping delicately from the shadows into the light, eyes glistening, nostrils drinking air.

And Robin remembered how he had tricked the Forester and how the starving man and his pale son had gone free. But there was something else, something forgotten, a nugget of sweetness which he had carried with him all his life without remembering it. A word in time to ferry him over the darkness that separated this life from the next. A name . . . The name the peasant had given to him before he ran free . . .

126

Age and weariness slipped away from Robin's face. His lips smiled slowly as the words surfaced from the depths of his mind.

"Master Outlaw," Robin breathed. "Master Outlaw."

"Aye, that you are," said Little John and tears welled in his eyes that had not known such indulgence since he was a child. "And Master of Sherwood, that you are."

Robin's breath rattled in his throat and he slumped back, dead, into Little John's arms.

They buried Robin Hood where his last arrow had fallen, and when the burial was over, Allan a Dale went on down the long roads of England, playing his harp and singing the ballads of Robin Hood which he had sung so often round the outlaws' fire. The wind caught up the words and sent them blowing through time and space – Little John, Maid Marian, Friar Tuck – and the magic names that echo in our dreams – Robin Hood and Sherwood.

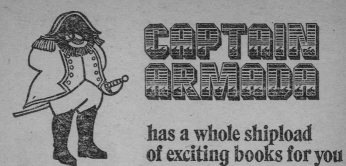

CAPTAIN ARMADA

has a whole shipload of exciting books for you

Armadas are chosen by children all over the world. They're designed to fit your pocket, and your pocket money too. They're colourful, exciting, and there are hundreds of titles to choose from. Armada has something for everyone:

Mystery and adventure series to collect, with favourite characters and authors . . . like Alfred Hitchcock and The Three Investigators – the Hardy Boys – young detective Nancy Drew – the intrepid Lone Piners – Biggles – the rascally William – and others.

Hair-raising Spinechillers – Ghost, Monster and Science Fiction stories. Fascinating quiz and puzzle books. Exciting hobby books. Lots of hilarious fun books. Many famous stories. Thrilling pony adventures. Popular school stories – and many more.

You can build up your own Armada collection – and new Armadas are published every month, so look out for the latest additions to the Captain's cargo.

Armadas are available in bookshops and newsagents.

Armada